LAST COOL DAYS

John Stewart

LAST COOL DAYS

ANDRE DEUTSCH

First published 1971 by
André Deutsch Limited
105 Great Russell Street, London WC1

Set in 'Monotype' Plantin
Printed in Great Britain by
Ebenezer Baylis and Son Ltd
The Trinity Press, Worcester and London

ISBN 0 233 96208 5

To
John Malcolm
and all the other young ones

It took the court two weeks to arrive at a verdict, and on the afternoon of August 18, 1952, Marcus was condemned to the island prison of Carrera. The afternoon was depressingly hot, and everyone in the crowded courtroom was sweating. The judge's dirty wool wig was damp around the edges, and from time to time he rocked back from his dais to dab at the long beads dripping down his black jowls. The police clerks and guards were stiffly wet in their coarse grey linen shirts. Even the varnished panelling of the room seemed to be giving up a little moisture. It was very appropriate that there should be an abundant outpouring of sweat in the narrow, high-ceilinged room this afternoon, for much labour had gone into the case of H.M.'s people of Trinidad and Tobago vs. Marcus Shepard.

As he stepped forward to receive sentence Marcus was sweating too, but his dampness was mostly concealed beneath the spotless white suit he wore. It was an elegant suit — rich doe-skin flannel, satin covered lapels, two inch deep pleats from the waist — and the well tailored fabric gave to his silhouette a defiant luminescence that could be clearly seen from the last rows back in the dim courtroom. Against the mahogany panels, the black and grey dress of the judge and court's officers, Marcus' black hands and head, had little configuration of their own. But the surrounding dimness was a perfect backdrop for his suit. And though he was slender, almost a diminutive man, his upright figure framed in such sharp relief by the white suit claimed the greatest respect that had been shown any prisoner that day.

The spectators, many of them housewives and idlers who had not missed a single day of the trial, were silent. Every eye was intent upon Marcus, all ears alert, awaiting the judge's decision.

Hille, who sat behind the balustrade separating the spectators from the dock and judge's dais, also managed to cut a defiant picture. Though not as luminescent as Marcus' suit, her face and hands were white. Her hair, honey blonde, sparkled with little flecks of light, but had wilted around the edges. Hille no longer tried to rescue the fallen damp streaks around her ears. She had already testified, and although she was not long in the chair she had sweated through her tan cotton dress at the back and under the arms. She had lost much of the poise with which she had appeared the first day of the trial. Yet, the rigid line of her body as she leaned forward, elbows propped on the balustrade, the fierce focus of her attention alternating between Marcus and the judge, resembled nothing in the spectators' memory of how white women behaved in public.

Marcus did not look around to accept the support Hille silently offered him. Nor did he look upwards to the judge who had begun his preamble. Marcus waited with his eyes dead on the panelled dais behind which the judge was half hidden, and from his stance, his attitude, one would hardly have known that his very life was about to be passed upon, that perhaps the time had come when he would lose it.

'. . . Marcus Shepard, this court after having deliberated long and arduously on the testimony offered in this case finds that it can only impose the maximum penalty applicable to your crime. The court recognizes that you offered no testimony on behalf of your innocence; but in the light of the facts of the case this could only be interpreted as another aspect of that nature which wilfully caused another man's death without the least provocation. Testimony has shown the deceased, Anthony Carrington, to have been a generous man, a benevolent man, and

8

one who befriended you even up to the day he died. The court, however, did not find full grounds for a conviction on the charge of first degree homicide. Instead, the evidence shows without a doubt that you are guilty of manslaughter, and the court so finds. Have you anything to say before sentence is passed upon you?' Marcus made no sign that he wished to speak, and the judge continued.

When the judge's droning voice came finally to a halt, Marcus had been sentenced to ninety-nine years and a day at hard labour. A few spectators groaned, many got to their feet. The trial was over, and the guard snapped handcuffs around Marcus' wrists. Hille cried. She made no attempt to cover her eyes, and her tears joined the sweat freely down her cheeks. She cried and many of the older women already on their feet had sympathy in their eyes for her — sorry, perhaps, that she was losing Marcus, perhaps pitying her for having ever known him. Marcus was himself now securely shackled between two uniformed guards, and as they led him past where Hille sat on their way to the cell block she tried to throw herself on him in a last embrace. The guards adeptly drew Marcus out of her reach and led him on down to the basement where several prisoners already awaited transfer to Carrera. The trial was over. The old men would return to their benches in the park to rehash the case among themselves — some denouncing the judge, others defending him. The house-wives would go home, or continue to their late marketing — some, in the pity they felt for Marcus or Hille, dabbing little handkerchiefs at their tears, others with a feminine vindictive-ness agreeing that 'jail was too good for him'.

At four-thirty Marcus and nine other prisoners were let out of their cells and handcuffed in pairs. Of the ten, Marcus was easily the most distinguished looking because of his resplendent white suit. It had not wrinkled a bit all through the long hours in the courtroom. The lapels lay back sleek from shoulder to waist, and the full cut pants bowed out in sharp creases all the way down to the top of his shoes. The other prisoners were roughly dressed in khakis, blue duck, or fraying serge suits. They might have come from the canefields of the south, the copra fields to the east, or the docks around Port-of-Spain. Two were Indian, six showed the mixed ancestry so common in Trinidad — African-Oriental, African-European — there was one other black like Marcus. They were all dark, with the mulattoes barely a shade or two less so than the others. Marcus was close to being the darkest of the bunch, but whereas the others all had either blunt or softly curved features, his face was long with a sharp nose and chin, eyes withdrawn deep into their sockets. His features showed an Ethiopian fineness. Not so the youngster to whom he had been coupled. This lad, clearly a labourer from the market-place, wore a sleeveless khaki jacket that barely reached the waist, no shirt, pants chopped short above the knees, no shoes. His round eyes, heavily muscled smooth black limbs hinted an Ebo ancestry. The dirt crusted on his arms and legs showed he had not washed in a long time.

As they were being marched out of the royal jail to the van that would take them to the launch at Carenage, a few of the prisoners made a show at being brave by talking loudly to one another. Others hung their heads, and marched with eyes fastened to their toes. Marcus had nothing to say, and therefore marched silently. But in his step there was nothing of gloom or bravado. He had no fear of Carrera.

When the prisoners and their guards emerged at the spiked gates of the royal jail in Port-of-Spain, it was raining even though the sun still shone above the clouds. The black asphalt road echoed the big drops that splattered down fast through the slanting light. Cigarette ends, dead leaves, bits of paper, empty tin cans, all the individual bits of debris which daily litter the city streets were being steadily beaten into the swirl of the open gutters. It was a sudden rain, violent, kicking up a loud noise against the street, the concrete wall around the jail, and the spectators who usually gathered along the sidewalk to witness the shipment of prisoners were forced to huddle beneath the eaves of the surrounding buildings for shelter.

The policemen were quick. Four guards with billy clubs ready hustled the prisoners into the waiting black mobile cage, another fastened the door from outside. There were no glass panels, no apertures through which the prisoners might see, and the few moments it had taken the guards to rush him across the sidewalk through the cloudy slant rays were the last Marcus saw of any sunshine.

In the courtroom there had been decorations, voices, and for many of the condemned an emotional stake in the juristic balancing between penalties and indictments. It was easy, for instance, while some advocate was summing up, or a witness being cross-examined, to ignore the sweat that dripped into the eye, the itchy damp shirt and drawers that drew roughly across one's skin. There were the witnesses — friends for, enemies against. The judge was up there with a face to be fixed in the mind's eye, a face against which in the future — vengeance. On every hand in the courtroom there was something to distract one from fate plodding its course with the greatest indifference to any individual wish or fancy. But inside the black van there were no distractions. It was oppressive. It was hot, and smelled of the sweat and tears of all the other prisoners who had ridden in it before from the royal jail to Carenage.

Once shut in, the convicts fell silent. They sat shoulder to shoulder on the bare iron seats in two rows facing each other, and the only sound that came from them was an occasional metallic rattle as one man or another tried lifting his manacled arm to wipe the sweat away from his eyes. The guards were more at ease. They sat in two pairs facing each other also, but once the van got started they removed their helmets and pulled out hand-kerchiefs to luxuriously wipe their forearms, and dab at their sweating foreheads. They made small talk among themselves, and neither of the four looked at the condemned men directly.

Marcus sat between a guard on his left, and on his right the boy to whom he was handcuffed. From his soft features the boy seemed not quite eighteen, but he had the muscles and frame which come early to those who labour beneath sacks of grain and provision in the market-place. He smelled of rotting produce and stale sweat, and the dirt from his bare limbs had already made smudges on Marcus' suit. The rain had left its mark on the suit too. Florin sized splotches were left where the drops had struck between the prison gate and the van. The lapels had become limp and wrinkled, and the creases that had stood so straight and sharp while Marcus faced the judge were now collapsed and withered.

It was barely a thirty minute ride to the jetty at Carenage, and as the van made its way up one, then down another of the narrow streets through Port-of-Spain, with the rain drumming against its metal sides, none of the prisoners spoke. But after they had made four or five turns, one of the Indians began to cry. He too was young, though not much of his features was visible between the long hair that covered his ears and cheeks, a moustache that drooped down to his chin. He sat with his head resting back against the side of the van, his eyes closed, and the teardrops that joined the sweat around his eyes slipped in quick succession down into his moustache. His cuff-mate, also Indian, but older, with a bald head and face wrinkled from many years under the sun, started a comforting song. The melody was dry as the windswept Punjab plains upon which it was first sung — a dirge. It was a hymn against despair that created a greater despair within all those who heard it, and after a while a guard lazily called to the Indian to shut up. The old man paid no attention, and the dirge went on, without words finally, a steady moaning in his high cracked voice.

Marcus saw and heard, but he turned his head away. He did not know what crime these men had committed, and he did not care. He had no pity to spare them, no commiseration to offer. As Marcus turned away from the Indian, his eyes met fully those of the black youth beside him, and the boy's soft lips twitched with the beginnings of a smile. Marcus hurriedly turned from that too, turned his eyes downward upon his splotched suit, away from all further contact with the men around him. He had no sympathy for anyone, wished none for himself. He was satisfied with his fate. If he felt anything at all it was only a subdued wish that he were already in the cell he would inhabit for ninety-nine years. But it was thirty minutes from the jail to the jetty, he knew that, and he mastered himself against being impatient.

At five o'clock the van arrived at the jetty, and a waiting guard unfastened the door from outside. It was a hundred yard walk from where the van was parked to the waiting launch at the end of the jetty, and the rain here on the edge of the sea was even more violent than it had been at the heart of the city. It came in thick slanting sheets, shutting out for moments at a time the narrow wooden pier, the dark moss-covered rocks over which the whipped sea foamed. The sun did not reach to land, and the wind coming down sharply through the Bocas not only threatened to behead the waving palms on shore, but had the small fishing craft anchored in the bay bobbing furiously in the choppy water. The corbeaux and seagulls that usually hovered about the fishing strip were absent. Yet along the sand on either side of the pier a few fishermen who were preparing their nets for another night's work moved like black ghosts in the grey afternoon. The narrow beach itself was the last bit of homeland before the launch, and while the guards marshalled the prisoners to cross it the rain finished in short time its soaking of Marcus' flannel suit. The gouging drops kicked up dirt on to his cuffs and drove against his coat until the rich doeskin became water heavy around his shoulders. And too, the rain stung where it struck his face and hands; and he had to squint his eyes to protect them.

The prisoners were formed into a file of five pairs before starting forward to the launch. Behind them the sun was shining up above, but Marcus did not see it. Had he looked back, he would have seen its pale afternoon band striking across the hills behind Port-of-Spain, just above where the broken rain clouds were trapped like fluffs of dirty cotton between the woolly green peaks. But Marcus did not look back. Across the bay before him Carrera sat somewhere out of sight behind the thick rain. He had no idea how long it would take for them to get there through the choppy seas. The tide was high and murky, and as he was being marched across the narrow spit of sand he caught glimpses of the black launch dancing high and low at the end of the pier. It wouldn't be easy boarding the launch, and Marcus grew a little afraid that he might get spilled into the sea. He was afraid too that the prisoner to whom he was manacled might do something stupid. From early childhood Marcus had heard stories of prisoners going berserk when they saw these last few yards of shore before them, and he thought perhaps it would have been better to return the boy's smile in the van. Perhaps he should not have turned away so abruptly from the fear which swam in the fellow's eyes. Now as they trudged out with the last guards some paces behind, Marcus wished he had spoken to the boy because he felt a trembling in the bracelet that bound them together. There was nothing he could do if the other decided to make a break, but follow. Perhaps he could just go limp and pull the fellow down before the guards shot. But that would ruin his flannel suit. The suit was already ruined, Marcus reflected. The pants, no longer with their creases, lapped sloppily about his legs, and the lapels of his coat drooped heavy with water. Yet if going limp wasn't enough, what could he do? The guards would shoot, and out of the grey rain the bullets would come smack into his sides, and he would be paralysed. Perhaps completely. Forever.

'Behave yourself, you hear!' Marcus shouted in the youth's ear, giving a vicious tug on the handcuffs. Then he was surprised at himself, for he had never spoken to anyone in such a voice before. All through the investigation, through the trial, he had not raised his voice once. The judge, Hille, the advocates and spectators, he had concealed from all his longing to be locked away.

But the boy did not respond. He walked with his head down, the rain driving heavily into his rough khaki jacket, and although his smooth muscled arm never ceased its trembling, he made no effort to escape.

Then, with the guard's boots still marking time behind them, they were past the last edge of shore, and as no fool would have risked jumping onto the oyster covered rocks which the tide intermittently uncovered alongside the jetty, Marcus relaxed into dealing with his fear of falling into the water when his turn came to board the launch.

It took a while to get everyone aboard. Two policemen clinging to its stern tried to hold the craft steady each time it rode up to the jetty's edge, and the prisoners leaped on in pairs. When their turn came, Marcus and his companion jumped without mishap, and another guard, after showing them where to sit, locked an iron bar across their legs. There was no cover to the launch. Rain and sea spray came in freely. The freshened bilge in the bottom of the boat was above Marcus' ankles. The men were all soaked, except the officers who wore oilskins, and although it was not really a cold day, the wind that came across the Gulf made Marcus shiver.

Once before when he had brought his geography class from the orphanage on an excursion, he had sat in the bows of another launch, much like this one, pointing out important features to his students as they sputtered beneath the northern straits . . . We are in the Gulf of Paria. Columbus, Sir Francis Drake, Abercromby, many historical figures sailed here. In the days of the buccaneers it was a haven for the pirates when they needed respite from their foraging on the seas. The Gulf, as you have seen from our maps, is practically landlocked. Twenty-five leagues south from here is the Boca known as what? That's right. The Serpent's Mouth. The channel through which Columbus approached after he sighted the hills we know as the Three Sisters. North of here is the Caribbean Sea. The narrow Boca which joins the Gulf and the sea is divided by three little islands that reach towards Venezuela — Monos, Heuvos, and Chacachacare. The latter, you know, is peopled by our leper colony. The straits around these islands are narrow and treacherous. Our frisky Caribbean rushes through in such mighty currents, this northern Boca is called the Dragon's Mouth. Just inside the Boca are two small islands — Gasparillo and Gaspar Grande — that stand in front of Chaguaramas Bay. Further south-east towards Port-of-Spain you can see the islands to which we are heading today — the Five Islands, or Los Cotorros as they were called in the days of the Spanish. The presence of these islands indicate that at one time, thousands of years ago, Trinidad was an integral part of the South American mainland. There, you can see the outline of Venezuela clearly. The islands of the Bocas and the Five Islands are rocky areas that survived the geological disturbance which separated us from Venezuela. There, that's the outline of Gaspar Grande. We can't quite see Monos. The Islands of the Bocas and the Five Islands have no beaches, no palm trees. They slope down at a very steep angle into the sea. In a little while we'll arrive among the Five Islands — and which is the most notorious of these five? That's right. Carrera. The rock prison. Very few prisoners ever escape its walls, and the few who do, either lose their lives in the currents or go to the sharks. In a little while we will pass alongside Carrera . . .

But that had been a bright day with the winds at rest and a high sun shining down from clear skies. A day with the palm trees along Carenage Cove rocking gently, glancing the sun off their bright green fronds. And behind, away from the beach, the hills beyond Port-of-Spain rearing up like monstrous woody humps beneath their matted green trees. Blue waves danced foam flecked across the Gulf, and bone-white gulls floated lazily above the fishing boats that were coming in with the late catch. From a distance the Five Islands themselves looked like woolly green humps, all except Carrera, which stood a stark tan-coloured rock with barely a tree or two silhouetted above the great wall. And when the excursion launch cruised past the island prison on its way to the Bombshell Bay resort Marcus had paid no more than passing attention to the towering ivory textured wall, the brass abutments like gleaming fists jutting out from it. That was a day of high sunshine, with many pleasurable hours exciting the imagination of his young charges. A day that ended with Hille waiting at the jetty when the launch returned to Carenage, in a sleeveless red dress that had no style other than what her slender body gave it. She had run forward to greet them, her head, her arms and legs as golden as the sun going down across the Gulf. And as she stooped to be hugged and greeted by the chattering boys her eyes smiled. They knew her for their most loving counsellor, and in a cluster they led her back to the waiting bus; the black hands which found no room in hers clinging to her skirt, the little black faces all turned up, each relating the day's adventure in its own terms. Only after they were all in the bus was she able to sit beside Marcus, and then her smile, the excitement she radiated, was for him. She surreptitiously stroked his arm and pressed her thigh against his, and Marcus, ever conscious of a few giggling boys, the Indian bus-driver who stared at them intermittently through his rear-view mirror, restrained himself from looking directly into her eyes. 'The boys had a good time,' she said. 'They all love you.' And after the boys were returned to their dorms Marcus was free to look as hard and as long as he wished into her eyes, hold her hand, and through the balmy night hear with pleasure all the little noises she could make over a kiss or other caress. In those days it was a great pleasure still to be with Hille, to stroke her hair under the moon, or sit through dawn with her watching for the sun's first crimson. Now all that was long ago. An experience in the dead past. And Marcus had no regrets. To arrive at Carrera safely was his only wish, and he worried that the launch would never make it because the captain at the wheel didn't appear to know much or care about what he was doing.

The launch shuddered and creaked with each wave and the further they drove from the jetty the longer the tremors lasted up the length of the craft. The waves grew taller, seeming at times to drive them backwards despite the churning of the twin motors. The sea came in repeatedly, and Marcus found it a useless job wiping the salt from his eyes. He was nauseous, and as they were time after time jarred and rocked, he had little faith that the labouring engines would get them through the rain that lay a pencilled screen around them. With one foot cocked up on the gearbox, the captain stood with barely his fingertips on the wheel, seemingly unperturbed by the storm. He seemed to ignore the sea completely as he carried on a laughing conversation with a companion guard beside him, while the launch kept wallowing up and down, stalling on the crest of each wave for a breath before smashing down again into the rough sea. In the end Marcus closed his eyes and silently cursed the officer at the wheel. With his eyes closed he knew that one of these times when they came down they would all go right under — the grinning captain with his hand so carelessly on the wheel, his companion, the two guards in the stern, and all the prisoners clamped to their seats.

But Marcus was wrong. The police launch took its beating by the waves, yet drove ahead steadily enough so that by five forty-five they were tied up against The Rock, and the prisoners were being marched up a metal stairway through the waiting gates of the prison. Some of the prisoners turned around for a last swift glance at all the freedom they were leaving behind, but not Marcus. He felt a great relief that they had arrived safely, that was all. Ninety-nine years, the judge said, and Marcus was satisfied. For ninety-nine years he would have silence, and perhaps, peace.

The gates closed, and the guards made a great deal of noise as they struggled with the chains and padlocks that fastened them. In the meantime Marcus and the other prisoners were marched towards a great iron-studded door that fitted into its archway much like the doors of Trinity Cathedral where Marcus once took his boys for a confirmation. There were no chains and padlocks here, the door slid apart as though under the magic of some unseen hand, and the leading guards took up posts on either side as the prisoners filed through. They entered a dim corridor, and when the cathedral-like door slid to behind them, the boy who walked beside Marcus began to whimper. One of the other prisoners up front was whimpering too, and Marcus felt a distaste for the whole bunch. For the ninety minutes they had been together he had looked at none of them closely, not even the guards. The prisoners were all just prisoners — ragged and dirty sufferers. The guards all wore the same grey shirts, black pants and white helmets on their black heads — they were all the same, servants of the prosecutors, the judge, and himself for ninety-nine years.

Once the door was shut, the wind and noise of the breaking waves were closed out. Not even the sound of the driving rain penetrated the deep corridor. The marching boots, the whimperings of the men who cried were lost in a deep silence that seemed to absorb all sound. Marcus was pleased. He would have been pleased to spend the rest of his time in just such a vault that gave back nothing — no reflection, no echo of himself. The snifflings of the others, the very sight of them made him anxious to be alone, and he tugged petulantly at the handcuffs which bound him to the whimpering boy. Would he have a cell with a view? Some life prisoners had them, he had heard. No cell could have much of a view, but something on a level that overlooked the wall, with a little window that permitted him to see the sunshine or moon on the water would be enough. And above all, Marcus prayed to be alone. He would not have his peace disturbed by another man, and if the authorities insisted on giving him a cell-mate he would pretend to go insane until they locked him in solitary confinement.

By seven o'clock that night Marcus had his wish. They had taken his fingerprints all over again and stamped a purple seal on the sole of his left foot. They had taken away the soppy flannel suit — Marcus did not care whether he ever saw it again — then issued him a pair of dingy underwear and a striped denim uniform. Marcus had expected that. As he had expected too he had to give his name over and over again to police clerks who filled out forms, and at the last desk they refused at first to believe he had no next of kin. But in the end the corporal who was recording that information gave up with a shrug and told him to pass on. By dinner time he and the other nine were completely processed and outfitted. They were marched into the mess hall which was the first room in the prison Marcus did not like. It was long, narrow and crowded. Hundreds of prisoners, it seemed, were crammed around two rows of tables lined up away from the walls. Two raised platforms, one near the entrance, another at the centre of the room, were occupied by armed guards. Other guards stood around the room behind the convict's shoulders. There were no windows, and the stench which struck as Marcus entered was a mixture of sweat and stale grease. The prisoners were all natives, blacks, browns, Indians, Negroes, half-breeds — with faces glistening from the humidity. And the general babble, the eating noises they raised to the low ceiling made it seem to Marcus that all the very noise and humours he had hoped to escape were crammed into this one room waiting for him. He was shown to a place, and he sat without making any contact with the prisoners around him. He kept his eyes lowered. He did not wish to attract any attention to himself, not did he wish to begin seeing the other prisoners as individuals. They were all there in convicts' uniforms, they were all alike, and that was enough for Marcus. He had no wish to know them or be known by them. He simply hung his head over the plate of rice and stewed fish that was set before him and ate what he could of it while pondering exactly how a convincing madman should behave.

Yet he had no need to perform that act. After the meal was over he and the other nine with whom he had come in were huddled off to one side of the room. A turnkey wearing sergeant's stripes and rimless glasses high on his black nose approached to read off their names and cell numbers, and as he read the prisoners were lead off in pairs between two guards. In place of the young boy, Marcus had for companion this time a bald-headed man whose black face had a kindly and compassionate air about it. The passageways through which they followed their guard were at first close and damp, and Marcus felt a sinking inside, for they were being led below. They went down well below to where no daylight had ever penetrated, and the ceilings were barely tall enough so Marcus could get by without ducking his head too much. As they hurried to keep step with the guard who leaned forward at a quick pace, the older prisoner jostled against Marcus, setting off his second outburst of the day. 'What's the matter with you?' he fumed. 'Can't you walk on your own feet?' The old man was panting, and behind his kindly face he was afraid. 'Forgive me,' he said. 'The floor is rough and I stumbled. I'm sorry.' The old man had not stumbled, Marcus was convinced. His jostling was a weak-kneed cringing from the lonely days ahead of him. He wanted to take the rub of someone along to his dark cell; and his apologetic manner made Marcus feel spiteful. Whatever punishment he was up for served him right, Marcus thought, even if he had committed no crime. He was the sort who believed in the world, who believed that to be locked away from sunshine and laughter was a mournful disaster. And whatever joy Marcus had in the past taken from being out in the world had gone sour. He had no compassion for the miserable old man trotting at his side, only contempt — and a dark feeling of disappointment because he was being taken into the bowels not the eyes of the prison. It would have been enough to see the sun come up some morning, to watch the full moon splaying off the irregular sea. Marcus was content to give up hearing, and seeing, and touching other human beings. He wanted silence, and there was not a pair of arms in the world he could think of without a visceral shrinking. Safe from any coupling in the dew grass, it would be a laugh on all the half-naked certain to be carrying on in the pastures and other places as if the moon belonged only to them. But how could he enjoy this new state if he were unable to watch the sun rise up sometimes?

The corridors grew narrower as the descent continued. The unplastered walls gave up, instead of echoes, little screes of sand that collected in heaps behind them. And at the fifth level which ended in a ragged cul-de-sac the turnkey brought them to a halt. There were three cells, each with a door of full length iron bars, and the weak electric bulb dangling above the middle door sent the bars back in solid straight shadows that blackened the interior of the cells. The turnkey opened the farthest door and jerked his head. The old man turned to Marcus with a deferential smile. 'Just you, father,' the turnkey said. 'Alone?' the old man asked. 'All alone, father.' The old fellow turned to Marcus again and tried another smile. This time, however, his lips merely managed a twitch, and his eyes stared hard as though they were trying to force some plea into Marcus' mind, but Marcus turned away. The guard finally prodded the old man into his cell and locked the door with a quick flourish. 'Peaceful night, father,' he said, and he with his partner started back out of the lower depths, marshalling Marcus between them.

In silence they retraced their steps, and only when they were past the main floor, ascending, did the turnkey offer, 'It's a dangerous business to be wise, eh? Old father is the smartest politician in the country, but all his brains get him is a dark cell. Much better to be a murderer, eh?' The second guard grinned, but Marcus made no response. 'For murderers the best cells are reserved. Did the thought of hanging frighten you during the trial?' Marcus was silent to that too, and the guard had nothing more to say.

It was a relief to be once again in the roomy, better lighted section of the prison, but after having seen the lower depths, Marcus would not let his hopes rise too high. At last they came to his cell. It was just what he wanted. The guard turned the lock upon him saying, 'Sleep well, my silent friend.' The metallic ring of the door echoed for a long time, but that did not trouble Marcus. He was grateful that the door was not made of full length bars. There were bars to be sure, fitted in a window through which he could look into the corridor, but the window was no more than a foot tall, and the light it let in from the interior of the prison made just a slant patch on the opposite wall alongside another window of the same size that overlooked the sea. Marcus could tell, for the splashing of waves against the rock came up clearly to his ears. He brushed between the bunk beds chained to the two side walls, and peered out between the bars of the rear window. The rain was over, but there was no moon, and he could see little in the outside darkness besides the lanterns of a few fishing boats, and the reflection from the lighthouse north above the Bocas.

Marcus stood at the window a long time. He watched the fishing lanterns dancing like fireflies in the night, and the revolving lamp at the lighthouse flashing yellow-red, round and round. He could not see the lights of Carenage, nor the glow sent up by the city proper. He faced north, and would never see the sun rise, nor see it set; nor would he ever see the moon again face to face. Never again see Hille face to face. Never again romp with his boys at the orphanage. And an end had come to all wandering nights beneath the cocoa hillside in Maraval, Hille's hand in his, her perfume distinct and more titillating than all the other essences of the night. An end had come to everything except seeing from a distance, and Marcus wasn't quite sure what that would do to him in the long run, but at the moment it meant peace — peace for which he had been so hungry so much of his life. 'Peace is death,' had been one of his grandfather's constant aphorisms, but even as a child Marcus knew the reverse was nearer to truth. Peace was life. Peace was being able to feel the life blood coursing in your veins with no need to urge it on or slow it down. Peace was feeling your heart tick, enough to rejoice in each contraction. Peace was living in the full knowledge of your fate, with a recognized end to the stretch of your days, and no anxiety as to will calamity fall today, or tomorrow. Peace, Marcus reflected, was after all a little bit like death, but not in the same way grandfather meant it. Grandfather was afraid of death, but Marcus wasn't afraid of peace.

There were things to be regretted. No more days promenading Frederick Street, no more days along the wharves sniffing at boats: from Grenada spices and goats, from Tobago mangoes and plums, from Canada saltfish, potatoes, and onions, from Argentina . . . from Brazil . . . Sniffing at boats and gazing at the ocean liners; gazing enviously at the departing voyagers high on the white painted decks, waiting for the steam whistle signal which set sooty tugs steering the great liners out to sea. Seldom Canada or Brazil bound, these liners invariably headed east once through the Bocas, and on a clear day from the northeast bay of Toco one could see them cutting the blue channel two or three miles off, heading for the open Atlantic, their red hulls dark in the distance, their funnels of steam darker yet arcing back against the sky and over their white decks. And pieces of Marcus went to sea with every liner, to Marseilles, Dakar, Liverpool, Cadiz, there to await the day when he would catch up and gather them all to himself again. No more dreaming: there was an end to that too. Yet the more deeply Marcus realized that he would never board a liner for anywhere, the more clearly he visioned ships upon ships cutting for the horizon, trailing billows of steam behind them; and he could not shut them out.

Nor did he want to shut them out. Later that night after Marcus had given up staring out between his bars and retired to the left bunk bed that hung from the wall, he continued to dream of the adventures that might have been his, the rediscovery of bits and pieces of himself in the wintry seaports of Europe, the jungles of Africa. For although Marcus had

24

seen no land save Trinidad, this island was only the culminating scene of his history. The spirit that possessed him was a mosaic of pieces from the jungles, the Mediterranean, the North Sea, all dumped together badly upon this little emerald of the Caribbean. Marcus could not sleep. He heard the waves splashing continuously against the prison rock: they invaded his peace. Even after all else in the world seemed at rest, the waves still came. They entered his peace, slapped at it, eroded it. They undressed him of the satisfied resignation he had known through most of the day, until he could no longer lay down. He jumped up to prowl the cell, but nothing new was to be discovered there — the solid bunk beds with their chains, the pails beneath, four warm and moist walls. Marcus kicked the pail, but its brief clatter was soon lost to the persistent splashing of the waves. And if Marcus were not a stubborn man, he would at that point have broken down and cried. But he clamped his jaws fiercely in the dark, and resisted the urge to throw his fists against the walls. The ships, the waves, continued their endless procession in his ear and through his imagination, and struggling against the melancholy, the despair of things that might have been, he prowled while the uniform grew damp with sweat that flowed from his head, between his legs, from every corner and crevice of his body. Then came a new sound, the echoes of leisurely footsteps, a guard stepping down the corridor, and Marcus rushed to the cell door. He grasped the short bars that prevented him from seeing too far left or right of the window. His fingers were damp on the metal, and sweat trickled down behind his ear. The echoes raised by the guard's footsteps were like a portent of some power to dispel all waves and far-off imaginary ships. Yet when the man came into view, pacing so close to the wall Marcus could have reached through the bars and touched him, Marcus saw that he was just a slender black man whose black and grey uniform hung sloppily about his waist and shoulders; and Marcus withdrew.

He returned to his bunk, and lay on his back looking up the

dark wall while the guard's footsteps reached the end of the corridor and started back. There were many things to be regretted — no more visits to the old village, the unfinished affair with Betty, the disgrace his family would have to bear. Not his family, just Grandfather who had been so proud of the boy that took right after him. Father was dead, and mother had disappeared — they couldn't be tainted by his disgrace. Grandfather was the only one who would suffer. He would cry over his rum, and the old men at the rumshop would pat his arm and be consoling — except those who took pleasure in recalling the boasts he used to make about the little genius that had sprung from his own blood.

Things might have been better if Marcus were really a genius, but it wasn't his fault that the old man started his boasting too soon. Marcus couldn't feel sorry for his grandfather. Nor could he feel sorry for Hille, even though he was aware that he had used her badly. It was not his fault; she asked to be mistreated. She even went so far as to want herself recognized as an accomplice in his crime. When the judge had pronounced sentence earlier in the day she had leapt to her feet crying, 'Murderer!' at the bewigged justice. And as the guard was leading him off in handcuffs she broke through and tried to throw her arms around him. Her wailing had disrupted the court, and the policemen were awkward as they tried to be gentle with her. But with all the spectacle she raised before and after the trial, Marcus felt sure that it was none of it for him. She never loved him. She was just a privileged woman who had ever been able to satisfy all her whims, except that of conquering him, and she was covetous. On those days when she had accompanied him on his walks along the docks, how she insisted on taking his hand! How fiercely she twined her pale fingers between his; and the more attention these locked hands drew, the more she swung them, flouted them in the face of all the curious and venomous stares. It was all defiance, even though she pretended not to hear the stevedores' murmurs, nor see the flicker of hate which clouded the white government officer's eyes, the malicious grins that spread across their faces. It was all defiance and covetousness, particularly when she yearned louder than he to climb the tall gangplank and sail off to any port on the globe at the cost of nothing more than a request to him. She was privileged. She had everything except a black skin, a slave ancestry, the confusion, deprivation, and melancholia that came with these endowments. And she was envious. She came from a race whose women had suckled the conquerors of the world. Shouldn't this make her all things to all men? When she lifted her skirts and lay down in the dry leaves upon the river bank in Maraval it couldn't really have been for him. It was not for him at all. The dry leaves crackled, cocoa blossoms perfumed the moonlight peeping down through the trees, the river played its little lullaby upon the rocks, and Hille performed in absentia. It might have been good to feel like a man laying down seed for a lifetime in that fecund atmosphere, but for that sort of thing a man needed a total companion, not Hille. Her little moans were no more than cries of distress, and with her a man had either to feel guilty, or take satisfaction in the baseness to which a woman could be reduced. That was her substitute for blackness and the despairing wish for vengeance which so many black men must harbour against the world. Hers was all self-inflicted. And despite all the rustling among dead leaves, creating a child with her never was a question, because it was understood that the limits of their bonding fell short of that. Hille was very aware of portentous disgrace. Yet this, finally, was Marcus' only true regret — that there was no son to make the journey of which he had dreamed all his life; no son to fill in the blank spots for which his soul would ever crave, give body and shape to the obscure fantasies that had made such a delirium out of his own life. A son would have been someone to whom he could explain his part in Anthony's death; someone to whom he could pass on the precarious glimmer into the depths of his existence which came into focus only when he had nothing else to do but die. And in time, Marcus reflected, he would have been much appreciated, long remembered. He had no sorrow for those whom he had unalterably left behind, but he lay oppressed with grief for the unconceived son.

Marcus willed himself to sleep away the encroaching despair and return to the few moments of peace he had known on first entering the cell. He ceased trying to penetrate the dark and closed his eyes. Sleep away the past, he told himself. Tomorrow, wake up with a fresh mind, a return to being at rest in this last cell. Tomorrow the sun would rise up from behind the hills, and he wouldn't see it, but he would have the laugh on Hille and all the others left behind who anticipated with the rising sun some new and joyous event in their lives. But Marcus could no more coerce himself into being cynical, nor could he lift himself beyond the reality of the night. Tomorrow the sun would rise, but not for him; nor would it ever again rise for him. The prison gates were chained. The sweating walls were real, the shark infested water slapping the rock beneath his cell a constant reminder that the village, the blue-green hills, the city would all see and feel the moon with no thought given to his defiance of it. He had been consigned to the league of forgotten men. And as much as he wished to forget and be forgotten, he could not prevent himself from filling the cell with those whom he had touched, or spoken to, or in some way dealt with in the past. He could not keep out Hille, bitch that he knew her to be. To have her breasts, what little she had, in his hands that night would have been a comfort. Anything. Her voice, her touch, her perfume, anything to tell him he was not forgotten. If only he could be sure that she was not at that very moment spreading her cloak on the ground for some other black man. But the night was void of all assurances other than the four walls and the splashing waves below. In the end Marcus gave up and clung desperately to every vestige of Hille's being he could conjure. He brought her close to him and let his hands remember the secret places of her bony body. He saw her eyes in the dark, the pale line of her cheek and throat. He felt her silken hair against his face. He remembered the perfume she wore the time they were together on the river bank beneath the cocoa hillside. It was a warm perfume that smelled so strongly of flesh with each whiff he took he seemed to be breathing her in. He remembered her hair smooth against his cheek, and her legs almost as smooth beneath his hand. Her thin arms, like a tight demanding bond around him, the clutching, heaving of her breasts against him, he remembered also. How her lips burned! And her tongue, striking his aside reached far into his mouth searching for a link, a trap, How she pressed! And searched. And if she were a big woman she certainly would have consumed him, but he had more muscle than she, and could lay into her, forcing her back onto the ground until every bone in her body yielded; and he had lost himself around and in her. In his dark cell with the shattering waves below Marcus remembered it all. He remembered the bones of her pelvis fighting him; he remembered how she struggled at the last and moaned, Marcus remembered, relived it all in the dim loneliness of his cell, even to the point where he felt his own discharge fly while Hille ground his ear between her teeth. Then it was over.

Sweating, his leg soppy in the coarse prison uniform, his penis bruised from rubbing against the corded material, Marcus rolled over onto his back with a little groan and lay staring up into the impenetrable dark about the ceiling. He was alone. Hille who never could stand being alone for long was not with him. He would be replaced. And although from the very beginning he had known the time would come when he no longer possessed her, although he had eventually succeeded in controlling himself so as not to desire the frenzied scuffling upon her bones too deeply, there lingered the uneasy feeling that whatever happiness might ever have been his rested in Hille. Marcus reminded himself that he had given her up for peace. Not only Hille, he had given up the village, the orphan home, the evening walks along the quay, everything for peace —

the indomitable peace of a cell in Carrera. Now he had that cell, but it was only the beginning. Before finding peace, he must first conquer loneliness, repulse the threat of regrets and despair. He must not let himself be swallowed. It was the first night, he told himself, tomorrow would be better. Tomorrow the pain of severance would have grown less.

Marcus took off his uniform, removed the sodden underwear. Then stretching out naked on the bunk, really willed himself to sleep.

Marcus was not at his window to see the murky quarter moon pass by at midnight on its way west; nor did he see the fishermen's lanterns bobbing furiously for shore when heavy black clouds obliterated that moon and stretched their fuzzy tails almost down into the water. He slept through the first hours of the storm, even though lightning intermittently relieved the darkness of his cell, and all Carrera shook under repeated blasts of thunder. And even if he were awake he would not have seen the liner come to a halt in the Boca nor hear the frightened cries of its passengers, because the rushing straits with their rocks, and channels made dangerous by the storm, were around the bend of Chagauramas Bay, completely beyond the view from Carrera. Marcus awoke at the hour of sunrise, but the sun did not come up that morning. The rounded peaks behind Port-of-Spain did not have the privilege of silhouetting themselves against any first pink morning light, for all the island of Trinidad and its surrounding seas remained dark. And if the hills were in any way distinguishable from the rest of the surroundings it was only because the rainclouds clung densest about their peaks, and the rain elsewhere as grey as the skies was greyer along their slopes.

Marcus awoke because someone was shaking him roughly, and a babble of excited voices filled the corridor outside his cell. It was confusing — not the rough hand on his shoulder, nor the babble of edgy voices outside his door, but the cylindrical barrage of greater noises that seemed to envelope them all.

In a daze, Marcus rushed to the grey streaks of light coming in between the bars of his window. It was not night but he could not tell what time it was. He held the bars and recognized the wind, whipping through the apertures, rushing in a tortured monotone above the noise of the sea. Thunder! Crackling from afar, exploding — as Grandfather so often said it would to rend the earth on doomsday. In the instant before the guard dragged him away from the bars he saw the lightning, beginning somewhere deep in the vaporous day and slashing down its blue tongue from the sky; the sea nearby, empty, except for the curling grey-green waves standing high, like a forest of restless monster serpents.

The guard shoved Marcus into the corridor where the other prisoners were waiting, and while he finished his dressing he saw they were seven from the previous day's ride to Carrera. The old politician and the marketplace boy were not among them. They were grouped in a loose circle, talking excitedly at the top of their voices. The young Indian who had wept on the ride to Carenage was the most voluble of all. His bald-headed companion whose face seemed familiar with all ages and seasons the earth had ever known was nodding his head, and gesticulating as he spoke. They were talking about the storm. One mulatto rolled his eyes, and emphasized what he had to say with sharp finger jabs into the air. It seemed, unlike Marcus, all seven had none of them slept their first night in Carrera. Each had lived through many storms before, but never one like this. This was a portent; and they were all so animated at the ominous explosions and rattlings around them they hardly resembled the group that had come in the evening before humbled and craven beneath their litter of individual miseries. 'You hear that?' the other negro shouted, pointing a finger at the thunder overhead. 'I'd just like to see that old judge now,' said one mulatto. 'Sitting behind all that varnish, with that musty wig on his head . . . I bet he thought he was really doing something, sending us to Carrera . . .' 'I bet he did. But old

31

Shango is going to send a thunderbolt that'll split this rock in two ... You hear that ... ?'

The electric bulbs hanging from the ceiling were astir, each following its own crazy pattern, and it took a second or two after each blast of thunder to tell whether Carrera was trembling its last, or whether the rock would settle down and face another crack from the sky. 'You hear that ... !' 'It sounds just like 1934 ... That was a storm! I remember the wind taking off the roof of our neighbour's house and blowing it straight out to sea ...' 'That's nothing. You should've been in our village. The church went down like it was made out of paper; and that was the strongest building in the whole village ...' 'I remember that. You remember what happened to all the big ships lined up at the wharf in Port-of-Spain ... ?' 'Not only the ships. How about the abattoir, and the fish market, and the customs house; the wind took all that down ...' 'That's right. And you should've seen those big ships out there ... smashing into one another, and turning over like tubs ...' 'That's just the wind; but how about the lightning? When I was a little boy we had a storm out in Diego Martin and the lightning split a big concrete house next to ours right down the middle. I remember because when we heard the noise my grandmother made us all get down on our knees to pray ...' 'Ain't no praying going to help if Shango decide to send his thunderbolt against this here rock ...' 'Man, this rock ain't nothing ...' 'It would go just like that ...' 'Can you imagine? That judge and all barristers and solicitors and inspectors sending us down here because they have so much faith in this rock ... ? 'Yes ... "Carrera is impregnable" ... ha ... ha ...' 'Impregnable my ass. Wait until the next blast comes ... We'll be out there swimming with all the carite and sharks — if we could ...' 'Ah, go on!' 'You want to bet?' 'Not this next blast, man ... I bet you three more!' 'Listen to Sonnylal. He wants to bet and he can't forecast nothing. Not even with a woman bawling it in his ear he can't forecast nothing; and he want to bet ...'

It was a great storm, and the men were electrified by the thunder and wind into an awareness of their own frailty which to them extended back to the judge, the courts and books of laws — the system that had been responsible for their imprisonment. Not one showed a sign of shame, none felt the need for repentance. They were altogether different from the broken bunch that had ridden the van and launch to Carrera, and Marcus for the first time felt drawn to them. They laughed at the jiggling light bulbs, pretended the floor was caving in each time it trembled; and while the guards were off rounding up other prisoners from their cells, this group of seven continued making wagers as to which streak of lightning, which thunder blast, would spell the end to Carrera. Not a grave face among them, they talked about the rock scattering into fragments without fear; as though their own deaths were hardly a matter worth considering. Marcus smiled at their antics. He looked upwards too at the crazy lights, and laughed after each wincing crash of thunder left them still alive, with merely someone having lost a wager. They were all in prison dress now, and really looked all the same. He was in prison dress too, and although he didn't really feel reduced to being the same as them, he had come nearer; though not so near as he had come to feeling his own purity, the purity of an elemental streak of lightning, or a thunderclap, or a blast of wind; the purity of any human being who has ever been able to stand naked and unmoved in the face of these things. And as he reflected, Marcus thought that really, the other prisoners had come a little nearer to being pure like him.

In time the guard had Marcus' group and another of similar size organized, and they started downstairs. The men fell quiet, and the word was surreptitiously passed back that all prisoners were being crammed into the lower depths of Carrera, where they would be protected in case the storm blew the top of the rock away. But once they reached the main floor they went no lower. They were led into what seemed to be a large classroom with a deep ceiling and heavy desks and benches running almost from wall to wall. The sixteen prisoners were seated, with almost as many guards behind their shoulders, and soon after, the chief warden came in. He was a short man, rotund and pink, with hair so light it could hardly be discerned in the dimness. His white linen suit was neatly creased, his moustache was clipped in a perfectly straight line above his mouth, and from his bearing the warden seemed obviously descended from that line of slaveholders who had along with fortune-making developed a certain gentlemanliness in the New World. His attitude was benign, his voice condescending, his eyes hard as blue steel. He called off the roll crisply, checking each prisoner with a stare designed to fixate him as a name — no less, no more. The warden cleared his throat after roll-call was over, and stepped around in front of the podium. He addressed the prisoners. 'You are all here at Carrera because of your various debts to society. Some of you have been a long time paying off, some of you arrived only yesterday to begin your instalments.' He paused. 'I needn't tell you that no matter whether you spend just a day or a decade at Carrera, when you return to Trinidad you will wear the brand of the criminal in the eyes of many. Such is life. Such is also part of the obligation you will have to bear for bringing yourselves here in the first place.' Pause. 'We have a storm.' A few of the men snickered. The thunder boomed, and the warden made another dramatic pause as though to let the weight of his observation sink in. 'We have a storm — a God-sent opportunity for each of you here to repay your debt to society in full, and earn once again the affection and respect of your relatives, your friends, and past employers; all those from whom you've had to be separated.' The room was quiet. 'This morning a liner bound for Liverpool was shelved in the rough seas as it attempted to pass through the Boca. I lately received word that the cargo will have to be rescued because the wind and waves threaten to send the ship down at any moment. A God-given opportunity for you to erase your debt to society

34

at a single stroke. All men who volunteer for this rescue mission will be honoured as heroes, and receive the full measure of the governor's attention that is reserved for heroes.' Pause. 'You have all been volunteered.' The men received their sentence without a murmur; and Marcus received it with a silent joy. Not that he cared about being a hero. Clearly, in a way which would have been impossible for him to articulate the previous night, Marcus knew he felt quiverings inside his shell. He was still pure; no wind, no wave nor thunder could change that. The warden's pronouncement was a challenge and Marcus received it as only a pure man receives his challenges — with neither fear nor visions of glory; with neither a wish to die, nor a wish to conquer; but simply a recognition that he was himself committed to an unchangeable shape, an immutable action that might be deflected but never denied. 'You have all been volunteered, and although the coastguard is at this very moment removing the passengers from the liner, we can't expect them to do everything. Someone has to save the cargo, and that's our duty. We will be outfitted with oilskins and lifebelts, and be divided into two launches that will bring us to the ship. Of course, any attempts at mutiny or escape will be drastically dealt with. We will leave now, under the command of Captain Gladstone.'

Although he had identified himself with the men in his speech, the warden disappeared soon after giving instructions to the captain, and the sixteen prisoners were led out to the launches behind Captain Gladstone. The storm awaited them, followed them. They retraced the very path that had been followed into the prison, but even when in that high-domed corridor which had impressed Marcus with its inviolate silence when he entered Carrera, the thunder followed. The prisoners were almost gay, and Marcus, feeling the thunder roll inside him, was filled with an excitement beyond any he had ever known. The men did not march in glum file, they hurried out in a chattering mob, and although Marcus had nothing to say,

35

he jostled along with the rest of them, his mind blank of all but the supreme ecstasy of the moment. Once more the cathedral-like door was opened, and the men doubled forward into the whipping wind and rain; and Marcus was with them, dashing for the landing post, the wind blasting his ears, the rain digging into his face and hands. Voices carried little in the wind, and directions for boarding the two launches tied up to the iron steps were given mostly by signs. The seas crashed taller than any they had seen at Carenage the previous day; but Marcus had little fear of falling into the water when his turn came to leap aboard. They were eight to a launch, and again Marcus had for companions the seven who knew the destruction of storms, who among them had figured Carrera no more than a bowl of dust should Shango direct the full measure of his thunderbolt against it. None of them was afraid. None grumbled or protested the warden's judgement in sending out two such little shells into a passage that had stoved a great liner. No leg irons this time, and no guards to hem them in. They were alone with Captain Gladstone, the same who had so nonchalantly steered them across to Carrera the previous day. As they rocked about in the tossing launch waiting to cast off, the old Indian who had sung the dirge threw aside his oilskin, and stood bareheaded under the pelting rain. Marcus did likewise. He wanted no protection. He unlaced the rubbery safety jacket that had been issued, and tossed that aside too. And when Captain Gladstone screamed at him, demanding with vehement gesticulations that he put it on again, Marcus laughed and kicked the jacket overboard. The captain with a petulant but helpless face turned back to his wheel. And as though this were a cue, the other seven all laughed, and threw their own oilskins and safety jackets to the waves. The men in their uniforms sodden to the skin, the sky, the Gulf, the atmosphere, all was grey, except Captain Gladstone off whose hunched back, covered in black oilskin, the yellow-blue lightning glistened each time it struck. The captain waited until the second launch had managed casting

36

off without being smashed against the rock, then skilfully he took his own craft away from the landing stage, across the crest of a broad wave.

The prisoners crowded around the iron rails and while the boat creaked wearily each time it was slapped from crest to trough, they held on. The second launch soon disappeared from view in the thick atmosphere and although the horizon had closed in to a mere hundred feet or so around them the captain, who knew his channels, stubbornly pushed the small craft towards the north-west passage beyond Chaguaramas Bay. Towards the Dragon's Mouth they pushed, for all that the foaming currents were doing to keep them out. The wind howled and shrieked like a chorus of wild birds, the waves cracked their wicked backs high above the prisoners' heads, but the captain pushed on. And Marcus, joined with the others in a discordant cheering for both captain and staggering launch gave no thought to the cargo they were on their way to rescue. He gave no thought to the tons of cocoa and sugar that would some-how have to be unloaded off the great liner, nor did he take time to reflect, as he often had in the past, that the sun-dried cocoa beans, the inanimate grains of sugar were more fortunate than he. They would cross the ocean. They would cross the ocean twice — first to the Old World as raw and separated elements, then back to Trinidad delicately integrated into savoury chocolate bars. A similar integration he had ever longed to achieve. He had several elements of himself in Trinidad, but they were fractional, and the missing pieces he had been sure were somewhere on the other side of the ocean. Yet out in the middle of the beating wind and rain, with lightening scathing ever nearer through the thick clouds, all such longing was forgotten. Marcus cheered as the boat leaned its edge into the water to skid through a trough then righted itself in time to breast another wave. He slapped the iron rail with a free hand and cheered the captain. The prisoners all cheered the captain and their craft, and although none had ever been to sea before,

37

each braced his legs and stood in whatever fashion he conceived true sailors adopted to face a wild sea. 'Ride, ride!' they cheered, and indeed they were riding, and Marcus was high as the rest of them, intoxicated with the danger of the moment, his own sense of facing it with no qualm, no hope, no reserve.

When Captain Gladstone put his launch into the entrance of Boca Monos they were in the most dangerous spot of all. The great wash from the Caribbean, overloaded through the narrow strait, threatened to sweep them back into the Gulf, suck them under, slap them against the high rocks, all at the same time. The launch dipped its bow, and bucked. It staggered, and spun around like a leaf in a maelstrom. The men waved their fists and cheered. Yet all rides come to an end, and after the captain had succeeded in righting the launch he shouted to find out whether anyone had seen the trapped liner. There was a lull in the cheering as the men also searched the rain filled seas around them for any sign of the ship, but it was nowhere in sight. The captain with his legs spread wide, his shoulders bunched over the wheel, managed with much manoeuvering to gain deep into the Boca, and yet there was no sign of the liner.

The men urged him on, for none wished to believe what seemed clearly indicated — that the liner had gone down. 'Farther! Farther!' The Captain glanced around, and it was written clearly on his black face that he wished to go no farther. He was afraid; for even on clear days when the Boca was relatively calm it was a frightening prospect to pass between these rocks and realize that the least error might leave a ship sliced in two upon their sharp edges. The captain knew where the liner should have been, and it wasn't there. He was for turning back but in the moment that he hesitated the engine stalled and the launch became a plaything for the waves. Crashing foam seas rushed it about, and sloshed it sideways in the narrow channel, while the men, their last shouted 'Onward!' just lost in the wind, stood open-mouthed and bedraggled watching the captain scramble to crank the dead motor. Over and over again he cranked, but the engine returned no more than a gasp each time and remained dead. Down on his knees in the boat's water Captain Gladstone swore, and he might have been crying from the frenzied edge to his voice. The prisoners did not cry. They had become suddenly helpless and the elan which had fired them a minute ago was gone with the wind; but they didn't cry. The two mulattoes fell down on their knees beside the captain and though they knew nothing about motors tangled their arms in his, yelling rapid senseless directions at him and each other. The hard old Indian held his head down in the rain and started up his song. The other Indians and the negro who had lived through many storms in his village stood mutely gripping the iron rails, as though willing the little boat to live again and take them on to the freedom which just a short while ago seemed within reach. For what other honour could the governor have bestowed upon them? Heroes! Rescuers of ten tons of sugar and cocoa beans! Freedom they had seen, glowing about the endangered cargo; and whether it were cocoa beans and sugar, the vaunted tropical products that had made slaves of their ancestors and empire builders of others, or salt, did not matter. Rescue the cargo and be free! No one had uttered these words, but as they stood silently bowed beneath the rain, Marcus could see the vacancy of a dying hope upon their faces.

The men no longer looked at each other. Their faces were set, and whereas in the beginning they had held the iron rails to prevent themselves from being tumbled about, here they gripped them as though they would through that connection establish their will upon the wild waters. It was clear — they wanted to survive and be free; and once again Marcus felt a rising rush of contempt for each of them. He had no wish to be free. Forgotten were his torments of the previous night, the regrets and loneliness. He was happy to be in the storm, and took excitement still in the danger around him. He was frail, he knew that. So let the lightning strike, let the waves smash him in and toss him up into the wind. They were all more powerful than he. And yet, once he stood his ground, indifferent and unafraid, they were as nothing. Here was oblivion in a moment, and here too were the finest moments of life, for Marcus stood on the rim of that oblivion with no wish to look away, no fear of leaping headlong down the deep chute of darkness, if the moment came. Despite his contempt for the others who hoped for life and freedom, Marcus too wanted the launch to start. Above all he wanted to continue riding through the Boca, out into the Caribbean Sea, out into any sea, as long as they were under the storm; but Marcus did not have his wish. For as a grey sea swept the launch high against the rocks of Monos the little craft shattered, and in a moment the wave had washed its fragments away. The prisoners and Captain Gladstone were scattered in every direction. One or two managed a gasping surge to the surface, only to be sucked deeper into the Dragon's Mouth and served up against the rocks on the other side. Marcus never came up. He went down with the first impact, and was sucked under forever.

In Trinidad the story of the lost prisoners became something of a tragedy, but one that was favoured less mourning than the loss of the liner with its cargo. Weeks after the storm was over, and the Boca settled down to its regular run of tricky currents, several merchants and shipowners still met diligently to plan for the eventual raising and restoration of the liner. But never an attempt was made to recover the bodies of the prisoners. It was generally construed that the currents must have washed them out to sea: and, anyway, if this were not the case, then the sharks had certainly eaten them.

Such was the end of Marcus.

In the beginning ... but to assign Marcus a beginning would be audacious. If there were a beginning, who knows where to find it? Marcus lived by invention. Invent or be dead. Perhaps a template of the first invention will in the future be discovered, but as of now, no one has the authority to assign Marcus a beginning. Subject to some compulsion during his last days, Marcus wrote down what he was about, and left behind a portrait. There remains that ... a portrait.

BLACK MAN, YOU ARE A BLACK MAN. YOU ARE A BLACK MAN. YOU ARE . . . What does it mean? Of course I am a black man. That's been settled long ago. I made that discovery long ago. What does it mean — you are a black man? To recognize your problem is to have it licked — half licked anyway. Doesn't matter that I haven't done much to figure out where blackness comes from, where it goes, what makes it want what it wants, what it means. Blackness has been ever since, and all the brothers and sisters gone before have hit on it. Nat, Douglass, Bessie, Billie, all hit on it, and they all scored. Butler, W.E.B., and Jack J. — not to mention The Lion of Judah — they all scored. There was something for me in each of their victories because blackness runs common among us, and while they were swinging for themselves they were swinging for me too, willy nilly. Sugar, Miles, Sarah, the way they wail, there isn't much figuring out left for me to do. All I have to do is BE . . . a man. I know. Walk through the village, Sangre Grande, Port-of-Spain. Walk . . . but how? How shall I walk? The posture I have lately assumed — back erect, chest out, arms spread, is defiant and aggressive, but tiring. The stooped shuffle of my grandfather, I spit on that. And on the second-class stomp. And on the pious mince of the martyr. And on the apprehensive trot of the criminal. I spit on every style of walking that demands I hold my body like an actor with ears cocked for cues as to whether I should cringe, smile, or be ready at any moment to take flight. How shall I walk in peace? What shall I do first of all with my eyes? Should I send them blind on the others around? On humped backs, broad backs, breasts, hips, feet? Should I concentrate on the empty space between the legs, or should I look up at the sky? Or should I walk hooded like the cobra — looking at nothing yet seeing all, ready to sink venom at a moment's notice? If I were not a black man, would I have such difficulty finding a peaceful style in which to walk?

YOU ARE A BLACK MAN . . . YOU ARE . . . A MAN! To be sure I am a man. I do not crave to live, I do not want to die. The problem was settled long before me. There are the anthropologists who proved I was no ape, the psychologists who established

42

I was not congenitally moronic. I have read the law-makers whose dissertations prove I am born free; I have heard clergymen announce that the same God who made Abraham Lincoln and Queen Victoria also made me. I am satisfied. The black colour of my skin is — incidental. We no longer live in the time when the black of my skin marked me as something less than human. The anthropologists, psychologists, sociologists, law-makers and clergymen have all gotten together and made me a man. I am satisfied. I am happy to be a man. Men walk upright, lesser animals slouch or go horizontally. Men have integrity. They are sincere, and they love one another. Lesser animals live by the law of the jungle. Men know God. They trust and share God. Animals . . . the distinction runs clear from earth to heaven. I am happy that the professional people-makers have agreed I belong to humanity. So why this refrain? YOU ARE A BLACK MAN . . . YOU ARE . . . A MAN.

Some revelation secretly matured of late? Trying to establish itself?

July 7, 1952

It is unusual to have a heavy rain such as we had this morning. It reminded me of rainy mornings in the village, sometimes with the sun bursting out suddenly to bring us wide rainbows. That didn't happen this morning I stood at my window and watched the clerks and labourers trudging down George Street beneath a dark sky, hunched up under their rain-cloaks and umbrellas. The music they usually make with voices and feet was lost in the rain, but none of them seemed discontented. Music did come from downstairs at The Undertaker's. His victrola was whining that old war song again . . . '*Rose Ann of Charing Cross . . . I'll keep your mem'ry ever bright . . . Rose Ann of Charing Cross . . . Dressed in a uniform of white . . .* ' I too might have been seduced by that song if my legs, like his, had been shot off in somebody's war. But I've never been to war.

The Undertaker is a white man without any legs who sits in

his parlour all day looking like a giant from the waist up. And if he catches you in a willing moment he would tell how he lost his legs fighting for the imperialist sons-of-bitches who never gave a damn about him, seeing as how he wasn't really a member of their club, only looked so on the outside. He was a brown man, he would let you know, brown through and through as the colour of his face and hands. Never mind his chest. He would let you know while his watery blue eyes remained unsmiling. Actually, his face is not brown, it is red. He is a white man. Redface. It is good I cannot hide from myself the way he attempts to hide from his. The black man in me is no stranger — is as familiar as the pain behind my eyes, even if as undefinable. I AM NO WHITE MAN . . .

That is a better song. More accurate. Never to forget, though, the white man coming into my life.

At one time he was unknown, unnecessary, an entity with which I had no need to reckon, and white, whenever that colour emerged, came either as clouds, teeth, a dress, paper. But in those days the table-top was also an entity unknown, and one with which I had no need to reckon. And as the table-top became a force with spoons, tall cups I could barely handle, the white man became a distant speck in the fields beyond our back door, different from the others there because it sat a four-legged horse quite tall above them hurrying about on their own legs. In time that speck took on a face — red, peeling, half-hidden in the shadow of a great sun helmet. A red face above white linen shirts and khaki shorts, and hairy legs clamped around the brown horse's belly.

'The Overseer' my parents called him. A man with powers far greater than any my father, or cousins, or my grandfather ever had. At his pleasure, I was told, we ate, had clothes and a hut in which to live. One casual command from him and we could be reduced to begging like the wrinkled old Indians who made their way through our village each day rattling the few pennies in their cups, crying, 'Alms! Alms!' Whether it were high on a horse, or behind the wheel of its jitney that sent our chickens flying in the dust, the white face was the same face — red and peeling, eyes that looked neither left nor right but straight ahead as though the water-woman, the dogs, my marble-pitching friends and I who scattered before its coming were somewhere outside its recognition. The white face — the Overseer. A man to be feared, honoured and respected from a great distance. A man for whom the front pews in church were always left vacant whether he attended or not; who after the last hymn was sung led his wife and sons from the church ahead of everyone else. The more intrepid liars among my crew boasted that the young redfaces were our secret friends. I was never backward as a liar myself, and one day when practically all of our surrounding cane had already been cut, and our village lay bare, denuded, at the mercy of the April wind which spread odours of boiling syrup across the open fields, I tried to give truth to a boast I had made as often as any of my bare-bottomed friends.

On an errand for eggs, I could take our village road to the Chinese shop, or cut across the rutted fields. The road was without adventure. With a lucky aim, my slingshot could startle nests of mongoose or manicou, sometimes even snakes, all the way across the fields. Doves too, cooing in clusters on the ground, hopping after worms that no longer had any protection from the sun. Where there were no animals, there was the wonder of the black-brown soil, which one saw so little of all the rest of the year, moving away mound after mound until it became the horizon. And at the end where a gully led out to the village centre, the dried up stream made a bed of cool sand scattered with marbles, pocket-knives and other treasures lost when the water had been high enough for swimming.

Coming back, it was a day for singing alone across the fields, and sighing too, in sympathy with the lonely palm trees of the next village; such tall scrawny leaning silhouettes in the bright sun. The two neighbour villages themselves, one saw them now — dark-green clumps of trees with whitewashed huts peeping through — and it was strange how close together they were once the cane had been levelled.

Between my house and me two boys were putting up a kite. A perfect day for kites — though I had seldom had a kite myself, and never a pretty one. Never one as tall at that which the two boys played. Didn't have tools to make good frames, never had money to buy pretty paper. Little redfaces struggling to put it up and the big pretty kite rearing then capping into the ground. I stood to watch. The kite needed tail, I knew, and after I had watched a while I set my eggs down on the ground and went over to offer that advice.

'We don't have any more cloth for tail,' one redface said. 'Do you really think tail's all it needs?' asked the other. 'Give it more tail, it'll fly,' I said. We then stood silent for a minute or so wondering how to manufacture tail out in the open field. Until the shorter boy said, 'Oh hell,' and started taking off his white linen shirt. Smaller version of the kind worn by the Overseer. 'Don't you dare!' cried the bigger boy. 'You know what mum said about getting our clothes torn. Besides we had to sneak one shirt already.' The younger boy paused, then following his brother's eyes he looked at me. Following their eyes I looked down at my ragged shirt, sleeveless, hung with falling away patches. 'How about your shirt?' the older boy asked. My shirt! The one of three I had. My play shirt, which had been last year's school shirt, and the year before my Sunday shirt. I made no answer, but my arms wrapped themselves around my body. 'It's awfully old, you know,' the older boy said. 'We'll pay you,' the younger one said, taking coins from his pocket. I wanted redfaced friends, but not at the expense of what I would get for sure if I returned home without a shirt. I turned and ran for my eggs, but they were just as fast as I, and as I had sense enough to be wary of stooping, we three stood around my eggs and the older repeated, 'We'll pay you. You can buy a brand new shirt.' 'If you give us the shirt we'll be your friends,' the younger one said. 'We'll be your friends forever.' His freckled red face looked over at me seriously. 'We'll give you money for another shirt.' Well, my shirt was old, and not worth much — against the possibility of having two redfaced friends. 'Will you really be my friends?' 'Cross our hearts.' 'We'll pay you.' 'You can come to our yard and play with our things.' Play in the redfaces' yard! Think of my ragged-tailed friends seeing me playing in the redfaces' yard!

I gave my shirt then, for how great it would be to boast, and truthfully, that two redfaces and I were friends forever. We ripped the hard khaki into narrow strips and gave tail to the kite. The boys let me have the coins from their pockets; and we three were off, zinging the kite, and soon it buzzed up into the sky like a pretty over-sized bird. The redfaces had cord enough to send their kite around the world; and when it was so high we could no longer make out the colours, we found a stake to which we tethered our paper aeroplane and sat down to enjoy it.

'What's in your paper bag?' the younger boy asked. 'Eggs.' 'What's your name?' from his brother. 'Marcus.' 'My name is Anthony,' he said. 'My name is Richard,' the younger one said. 'Are you really going to buy a shirt with the money we gave you?' asked Anthony. 'I'll give it to my mother.' 'Will she buy a shirt with it?' 'I think so.' 'She won't buy any shirt, I bet,' Richard said. 'Father says you people spend all your money in the rumshop.' 'That's true,' Anthony said. 'Our nanny's always drunk. What is your father's name?' 'Herman.' 'I bet he drinks rum all the time.' 'He drinks and comes home staggering drunk, and beats your mother,' Richard said. 'Father says you people do that all the time.' 'I don't think you should take our money,' Anthony said. 'It's my money! I gave you my shirt for it.' 'We have no right putting money into the hands of drunkards, father says. Give it back . . . ' 'No . . .!'

Prepared as I was, I was no match for two — because I was mostly prepared for flight. Anthony blocked my way, Richard kicked my legs, and I fell. Came up with dust in my mouth, and tears, but didn't strike back; for what was the use? Redfaces were powerful, far more powerful than the four balled fists I faced. The immense calamity which angry redfaces carried around just for dropping on people like me made me weak and trembling inside. I knew it as well as I knew the deadliness of the

47

steam locomotive that hauled cane. I had never been run over, nor seen a worker run over, but I knew that if ever I was trapped in the tracks of the steaming iron charger there could be no survival. In the end the redfaces got their money back, and I got my eggs splattered up against my head. At home, I got a whipping from my mother — not so much for losing the eggs and my shirt, but for, worst of all, interfering with the Overseer's boys.

My bare-bottomed friends laughed. Each time we met for marbles, or a game of cricket, they laughed and had a good time throwing imaginary eggs at my head, or offering me fistfuls of paper coins. And what could I do? Dream of vengeance. Long for vengeance, going unfulfilled no matter how many nigger heads like mine I whipped. Ah! Even as my knuckles messed up another pair of black lips, while I'm tasting blood from my own loosened teeth I would be understanding 'this is not enough'. White blood. Rage. White blood. To feel my knuckles into a real redface. Feel his flesh tear. Hear him groan in pain. I had to have that. Nothing else would do. Dream inherited from my race, nothing else would do. My father, Grandfather; coming into their dream and a determination of my own that didn't know what next to do besides whipping black heads and waiting.

I know now it must have been this same frustrated blood call working itself out in my father, times when he ducked his head at the mention of the Overseer. He never had many words for me, but always the consistent reminder that I was 'a little black boy'. Would it be enough to say that he lived in fear? Fear of himself. For why else would he have grown numb? It took rum more than anything else to arouse him, and Saturday nights when he came home drunk he would be full of plans for our future. His moustache bristling, an insanely determined look in his eye, he would explain exactly how next week he would patch our hut against the rains. With much ardour he would caress Mother, recalling the time when she was the sweetest girl in the village, and promise her a trip through the great department stores in town to buy dresses and shoes of a style never

48

before seen in our village. He would agree when she said he drank too much, and after counting up with her all the shillings that could be saved if only he would learn to by-pass the rum-shop, he would vow having had his last drop already, and in his dreams convert all the shillings thus saved into more dresses and hats, and shoes for the boy. He would promise me things too — a bicycle, trips to the theatre, that he would see me enrolled at the town high school after I finished seventh standard. And in the beginning I had faith in his promises. I believed him when he reeled off our heritage—illustrious descendants of ancient African royalty — all the way back to the Mundi of Mandingo, and vowed that he would see me a little Lord in my own right before he died.

A long time passed before I realised that he never remembered Saturday's promises on Sunday, before I understood that he knew his dreams to be futile and the ritual of Saturday night was simply that — ritual — and never intended to be anything more. It is only lately I have come to understand that he must have been sharply aware of his short-lived madness, for I have been hearing again the songs he sang and played on his guitar to close out those Saturday nights, and each chanty — I hear them now—laments the passing of his foreshortened fire. His personal bereavement.

Mother was not an impatient woman, nor was she a hag. She asked for little, and was neither happy nor sad at the outcome of her wishes. She took her drink at home, and the rum made her more quiet, She too laboured in the fields, but she never complained, nor like some other village women pretended to have accepted her fate. She insisted that I attend church but never went herself. Sometimes she sang alone, but never did she sing with Father. Saturday nights, after he was through with his fondling, his promises, and had retreated to his guitar, she swept the floor or smoked on the front steps if there were no rain; or if it were raining she emptied the pans which caught water from the leaks through our rotten galvanized roof, and washed herself in the corner before going to bed. I remember her as implacable; yet she must have had at least one secret wish festering behind her unrevealing face, for after Father did what must have been the only thing he could do to save his life, she was just as swift to save hers, and I was left alone.

I was sad but never cried at my father's disappearance. I knew — although no one said so — that the redfaced Overseer had something to do with it. The morning Mother and I awoke and found him gone, she took a careful look around the hut to see what else was missing. I helped her. We never had much, and it didn't take us long to find out that he had taken nothing but his guitar, the khaki suit he must have been wearing, and his only pair of shoes. Mother said nothing. She went to work in the fields, and I went to school. That evening she came home and cooked supper. Then with me waiting at the hut to see if Father would come back, she went to the priest, or so she said, him who was the adviser of everyone in the village — sinner, non-believer, church member, or else — in the time of trouble. Mother went out to the priest's, and she was gone a long time while I waited, and finally fell asleep alone.

In the morning when I awoke to the grey light coming through our dingy curtains my bones knew immediately that I was alone. Our hut was too quiet. I sensed a bleakness in the atmosphere even before I saw that Mother's two pairs of shoes and her dresses were gone. Father gone, Mother gone, I was alone. I remained lying down a long time, and afterwards I did not touch what little food there was in the cupboard because perhaps if everything in our hut remained just as it was before they left, Father and Mother would return, and the dream state, quiet tension in our house would be over. I remained in the hut two days, waiting, listening past the rumble of the sugar factory, the clatter of mule-carts hauling cane; listening into every voice, every footstep along the road for something that said 'Father' or 'Mother'. And then Grandfather came and took me away.

He cursed a long time, beginning with the day my father was

born, and called my mother a sly slut. I didn't like him saying that. He gave me a room in his house, fed me, and made me sit down to a drink with him. 'You're thirteen years old,' he began. 'Your father and your mother have disappeared, and you think your world has come to an end. Let me tell you, when I was your age I couldn't remember what my mother looked like, and I was already earning my living in a country hundreds of miles from where I was born . . . ' I had heard Grandfather's tale several times before, but the bookish style in which he told it always captured me. Grandfather had a way of using words that made all the dead scenes in my history book come alive: Bridgetown, Castries, St George's, he made all these places come alive in my imagination as bright, rough, sea-washed towns with rogues and labourers, always managed and man-handled by redfaces.

These ports of Grandfather's childhood teemed with tenacious creatures like himself — not the arrogant European admirals and pirates of a past century. Belize, Panama, Cartha-gena, he gave them sunshine and suffering, rain, leaky huts, and fights along the wharves; scrappy women and malicious men, and the ominous redfaces forever hovering in the back-ground. Grandfather's words gave each place its due smell of fish and rotting bananas, the taste of dirt through the nostrils — brown, black, red dirt — and left me with an unspeakable wonder at his having been able to survive despite the countless gallons of sweat, the litres of blood he had left behind. How could he have survived the brutal starving passage on some little sloop from Kingston to Demerara? How could he have survived the tons of sugar-cane, cocoa beans, copra and bananas that had ridden his shoulders from so many wharves into the holds of Europe-bound vessels? The treacherous compères who broke his leg so they would have one less loader in competition — more money for rum and saltfish among them; the black starving women who gave him two minutes of disease for a week's pay: the squalor, the violence, and above all the omni-present redface who saw to it that each day he was worked to within an hour of his life; how did Grandfather ever survive all this? His grizzled face hinted an answer. He was dry and wrinkled now, his walk was stooped, yet the signs of deterioration were countered by a glitter in his eyes. If anything about him offered insight into the secret of his survival it was his narrow black eyes that gleamed with all the slyness of an old mongoose. And his words, 'Self-confidence and dignity son. You've got to keep hold of those two no matter what happens. You've got to know what you can do and do it the best way you can without losing any uprightness.' Self-confidence, and dignity. That he told me was how he was able to outlast the decades of scuffling, the numerous little one-sided battles that had warped and twisted him into the dried-out prune that he was. And I had to believe his eyes — they swam with wisdom. I had to believe his eyes because whenever he talked to me of self-confidence and dignity there was mirrored in their glance something as old as the race and just as immutable.

Grandfather was one of the few villagers who had some property to show for his years of toil. He did not live in a hut provided by the sugar company. His plot, on which stood breadfruit trees, plum, and cedar scattered in a formation cast by the wind and errant birds, was half an acre wide. The house, a big grey skeleton of rotting boards, low and dim inside, let in streaks of sunshine wherever he had failed to plug the crumbling seams with rags or old newspapers. The galvanized roof was blistered with rusty welts that cracked in the heat or strained raindrops through a storm. The furnishings — tottering chairs and tables, musty beds, were all surrounded with an odour that said 'Committed to dust. Beyond revival'. Self-confidence and dignity were surrounded by odours of the grave, but not yet dead: lived on in two ancient, glittering eyes. So, old age and the tropical weather were about to overtake him; but his death would be no defeat. The pillars of his house were decayed, whatever laughter once fell into his rooms had long since passed on, but behind his eyes Grandfather had it still. He had the voices of those whom he had outlasted, the laughter of his women. The smell of tar and sawdust, and the feel of raising his roof with his own hands. Behind his gleaming eyes Grandfather had all those memories attesting to his confidence, his self-assurance, his manhood. He had survived the struggle, so when I was thirteen it did not matter that Grandfather had come to our village in his thirtieth year with enough money to buy his plot, build his house, and that for forty years afterwards he had been able in no way to fend off the decay that leisurely swallowed up his labours. It was enough that this old man so old, so spare and dry, had seen the world, had dealt with it since twelve and come through successfully — alive and with all his senses — powered by his self-confidence and dignity. It was reassuring that such a thing could be done by someone whose blood I had inherited. Very comforting to know that dignity and self-confidence were integral parts of my own makeup.

Many years went by before I awoke to the realisation that Grandfather was unique, I was unique, and whatever resemblance we bore to each other physically was no proof that we had been cast in the same mould through and through. Grandfather had the facility of being able to bow his head low and still remain upright. He had suffered many redfaces to kick his ass day in and day out with no retaliation, or with all retaliation bound up in his self-confidence, his supreme dignity, his faith in eventual survival. Father also knew faith, but knew it only when there was no sweat in his eye, when his imagination had been released through rum from the tight corral in which he kept it. So he escaped. Ran off. 'Gave up,' Grandfather said, because he never learned how to bow and remain upright at the same time. When he bowed he was truly humbled. Couldn't play the game. Didn't have any endurance. So he walked away from the Overseer, the hot fields, the village, taking nothing with him but his guitar.

As for myself, I do not wish to survive if survival means being grounded in that terrible decay of my grandfather's. Neither do I wish to escape, if escape means only the fruitless nomadic wanderings of my father. We heard about him — stories of a drunken, filthy man who hoboed from village to village, an unkempt skeleton of a man whose only grace lay in the music he made with his guitar and his singing voice. I want escape, I want survival, but not their kind. Rolled into one. I have always wanted escape and survival rolled into one, although at thirteen I didn't know how to say this. But Grandfather must have known. He must have seen his early self in me, and in the beginning that was what he wanted too. And being a man of faith, he encouraged me: 'Have faith boy. Dignity and self-confidence. Have faith in what you can do, and you'll do it.' And as he spoke I imagined myself fearless before any redface, fearless within any circumstance; but at the same time the dryness, the decay that filled his house was strong in my nostrils. Yet, Grandfather fully at ease in his wizened age, immediately set a plan. He would, with money no one suspected he had, hidden in an old hat, see me through the town high school, and the only provision I had to fulfil was that I be the comfort of his old age. He would give me his eyes, provided I let him look through mine from time to time. He would give me his support, his wisdom, provided I let him refresh himself in my dreams. With a child's cunning I hid my gladness, but Grandfather's plan made me happy. Particularly that part about going to school in the town. It would be a start. Towards survival, peace, a healed soul — which, even then, I understood in my blood would, in combination, be a rare achievement.

July 7, p.m.

Hille and the reverend-tutor might have been good for each other, had they ever met. Masculine maturity and great knowledge of the world on one hand, on the other, feminine super-stition and frailty. Both romantic adventurers. Both driven sojourners in a foreign and to them exotic land. In search of what? The reverend never said, but I can see now we temporarily gave new life to his pulse. Not we, Betty. Her rhythm drove his

54

blood so fast, it took away his choices and forced him to debase himself. Until she became familiar. Then he had to move on — and I cried to see him go. Move on. Quicken the pulse, absorb, move on.

Hille, not as seasoned as the tutor, has trouble moving on. On my way back from tonight's walk if I had not spotted her lurking beside my steps before she could see me I would have had no alternative but to bring her upstairs, and I don't know what then I would have said to her. She's still caught up in fancy. When we first met, she found everyone at the orphan home 'charming'. Unexpected afternoon storms 'sent her', and she was just enchanted by 'all the colourful wildlife'; meaning our everyday shrubs and gardens. In the village, our drunken men and high-hipped women, she loved their bodies. The way they walked . . . Oh, so lovely! 'Aren't they just lovely, Marcus? Such natural grace in the way they walk — like dancers. I wish . . .' Mistaking what was to me a thirst for blood. Her blood. Blood of others like her who kept themselves remote and sucked on us. So much of it before her, and she, voluntarily suspending kinship with the redfaces who sucked life from our village not even suspecting. A thirst for vengenace consuming the thirsty — she called it lovely. From childhood I used to hear the sighs go up at dusk, and watch our women who having loaded sugar-cane on their heads all day come home to stoop before the fire and mechanically turn out another meal (saltfish and rice) with mostly abrupt harsh words for the children, often no word at all for the husbands. The men, too, seldom had many words for their women. And if the children laughed too easily, or in other ways enjoyed a merriment which the grown-ups couldn't share, malevolent eyes, a harsh voice — SHUT UP! Nights were for nursing weary backs and fagged out hearts; for generally pulling the spirit together before another tomorrow. All around the houses and yards, about the public school, the church, the shops — wherever the village air thickened it smelled of dried sweat and coming decay. Everywhere was that odour of men who laboured too hard, that stench of men and their buildings decomposing too fast. Were I a man then, I would have wanted to cry, 'Stop! Fresh air! Let me see where I'm going!' But I was not a man, and all I could do was let myself choke with an unspeakable sadness at the exhaustion and swift decay that seemed certainly in store for me too. Even for those workers who during Lent placed themselves in the church's keeping five times a week (at other seasons less), relief was a mockery. The church itself sat right on the edge of the canefields and as the choir raised its passionate hymns to a long lost saviour, the dry cane stalks rustled in accompaniment, rustled their own suffering unto death with a more sustained voice than the congregation. There was no escaping it. Redface had decreed — the days for labour, the nights for recuperation.

In the early morning, voices joking, cajoling their way to the fields and factory came like dry bells that had lost all sweetness. I saw and heard. The days were hard, the nights painful; and Saturday night, the night of spree, was filled with its own pain, its own grotesqueries. This was the night of rum, blood-pudding, quick fights, and heavy vomiting under the gas-light of the Chinese shop. For women, a weary time of haggling over rice, lard, flour, and pickled meats, then going home to await a drunken husband's pleasure.

And after the Chinese shopkeepers had won their high prices, and at eight o'clock all the drunk and dying were kicked out, the shop turned dark, our goatskin drums commenced their rattlings in every quarter, dry voices went up singing calypsos or Hindu chants. Watch the drunk men stupid blind stagger through the dark. How very lovely . . . All the stoop-shouldered dried-out black men getting drunk in a village shop, their bare feet in puddles of warm vomit, their fingers clasped around glasses of rum the bottle-green flies sipped almost as fast as they. Lovely! The sack-dressed barefoot women haggling over spines of codfish that had been spat upon somewhere in Nova Scotia then kicked across the sea in splintered barrels. The squabbling, the ragged songs, the wailing; the smell of sweat and rotting pickle; how lovely the light-headed men weaving their way through the dark high on a rum vapour, and the women who either rendered body and soul or got their faces bloodied. Like dancers. How thrilling the lithe, the supple twisting of the dancers; how simply primitive and pure and exciting. How simply exciting! But Hille never quite understands much of anything. She is in some respects short-witted like the tutor who came to the village during my fourteenth year. He, a redface, with grey hair cut short, like bristles on a young hog. Never without spectacles, and although far from robust walked like a soldier on the way to victory. This, combined with a grimness about his lips and eyes (like photos of Kipling or Teddy Roosevelt) had us all thinking when he first came that our new priest was a man to be reckoned with. That's what the tutor was — a priest. One of those white-frocked men who somebody in England said should come to our village and soldier in the field, ostensibly for the Lord. Soldiering done mostly for everybody but the Lord — and the natives. But in those days I was concerned still with being a 'good' boy, and the tutor appeared a guide. An able sojourner, as the old women called him — a storehouse of knowledge and wisdom, as I came to find him.

The Reverend had been a traveller. He had travelled Greenland, Europe, Asia, Africa. Had seen it all, traversed all these lands with his own feet, spoken strange tongues with Eskimos and Hottentots. There was not much in the way of human customs he had not encountered. It was therefore very flattering to have him stroke my head after our harvest-time cantata and say, 'Wouldn't you be a prize in England?' I had read passages from the bible and sang —

> Be not afraid, ye beasts of the field
> Be not afraid, ye beasts of the field —
> For the pastures of the wilderness do spring . . .

and later he had come into the vestry where we choir boys were taking off our cassocks and surplices. 'Well done, lad,' he said.

Harvest time, the church hung with palm fronds and fruit. Oranges, golden-apples, coconuts, dried corn. Everywhere evidence the earth had been kind to us another year. Citrus blossoms and wreaths, pink lilies, their sweetness bringing home the smell of God's living grace, bringing it all the way into the vestry where the air was otherwise damp with the smell of stale linen and incense. Our shadows from the two thick candles high on their carved stands upsliding higher than the guild banners furled in the corner. 'Well done, lad. Reading as well as you do, wouldn't you be a prize in England?' In a voice that let everyone know I had suffered a great misfortune being born in our village.

I loved our village. That is, I had even then already cried in each of its corners. My salt was everywhere intermingled with the earth, the trees, the grass that took their food from the ground. From the corner where the red Anglican church guarded our village burial ground, past the school, past the brown pine cottages of those workers whom the company had favoured — brown with wear and weather and barely saved by narrow traces from the canefields raging up to their back doors, but better than the huts and barracks to follow; and before the huts and barracks a narrow square enclosed by the rusty post office and general store, Charlie's rumshop, a Catholic church in bright red brick, the stuccoed police station pink and black; then the bridge — singled-railed, too narrow for more than one mule-cart at a time — and alongside the factory waste-stream over which it stretched the huts and barracks, rank on rank — rusty galvanized eaves coming almost to the ground — homes of the poorest workers, whitewashed, but fetid with the smell of too much living in too little space; past the bridge to the Methodist church — the last gate-keeper of the village — grey-walled, far back from the road, with gnarled fiddlewoods and tufted palms solemnly clustered about it; and across from the Methodist church our pavilion which the company had so graciously donated the village. I had cried over our dead in each of the churches, and at the rumshop too — over the fallen but not dead — and even at the pavilion I had cried, here without explanation. All between these churches where our village lived, with the stinking waste-stream never quite a full smell away, I had cried and bled and pissed long before the Reverend ever came. But it took his coming to see me into the fresh green and white bungalows of the redfaces beyond the Methodist church, beyond the great sooty factory that was meeting ground for ourselves and their colony clamped down on the grassy hillsides around our pond. Beyond the bridge, beyond the factory that was a mile from the bridge, the redfaces who were responsible for the factory being there in the first place, the redfaces who ran the factory and therefore needed no other weapon to run the village, were safe from nauseating odours, niggers, and coolies alike — until the Reverend came.

He was in the village only a few months when he had us — the acolytes and members of his choir — admitted to the Overseer's house on the third night before Xmas to offer up carols. Never before had I been in such sparkling rooms. There was no smell of decay here. The floors were polished, the walls were solid and clean — painted in pastel colours that reminded me of candy and sweet things that were rarities in my life. The furniture was even more highly polished than the floor. There were no holes in the chair bottoms, and the tables seemed certain of the legs upon which they stood.

I sang carols in Anthony's house on the third night before Xmas that year, and no one would have guessed that he and his younger brother were the same two who had tripped me up one day the year before in the fields and stolen my shirt to make tail for their kite. None would have guessed it, but I was so intent upon them I never even paid much attention to the Overseer and his wife whom I was meeting up close for the first time. I remember the Overseer's legs were covered in grey flannels, and his wife, a broad-bottomed horse-faced woman — who village rumour said was in the tropics to get rid of her TB —

sat with her hands clasped in genteel fashion, and her lips drawn back from her horse teeth in a grin that lasted the whole time we were there. 'Very well,' the Reverend said, as the choir semi-circled around the room, and after each part had sounded its note the singing began.

Although Anthony was the same age as I, and his brother Richard just two years younger, they sat like redfaced cherubims in white linen shirts and school ties, deep in the enfolding softness of their leather couch between the Overseer and his wife, accepting benignly the music and little drama we made. I was a king, scrawny and black, but nevertheless a king, bringing gifts from the Orient to the baby messiah — my divinely crowned ruler whom I should ever serve. Anthony looked on with a condescending grace, accepting, and at the same time beyond gifts, pleasures, or whatever else I could have to offer. Yet I was a triumph laying my gift at the feet of the once and ever king —

> *Myrrh is mine, its bitter perfume*
> *Breathes a life of gathering gloom;*
> *Sorrowing, sighing, bleeding, dying,*
> *Sealed in the stone cold tomb . . .*

The Reverend applauded, the Overseer and his wife applauded, and so did young Richard. Anthony did not. He remained unavailable. Even as he served dates and other delicacies at his mother's bidding he did so without a smile, with only a self-contained absent look on his face, as though he was spiritually cut off, I came later to find out. He looked to me as I would have liked to look to him — aloof, capable of direct appraisal — but I was already conditioned to the oblique and saw him from left, from right, from underneath, but never straight on. I should have been pleased and happy, I suppose, as along with the other 'kings' and chorus I was entreated to sit in the soft leather chairs and eat the Overseer's imported fruit. A large part of me was happy, but Anthony's presence rested heavily on me. He seemed to comprehend the conflicting feelings I had about him, and I couldn't tell whether he was hostile or indifferent to what he recognized. Did he know how much I wanted to smash his face? Did he care that I longed at the same time to have him for my true friend, to feel comfortable in his father's house? Did he understand that the fear through which his father ruled mine was already alive in me but that I was determined to fight it off! I couldn't tell.

The Reverend was pleased. He applauded his troupe and praised the host, trying all the while to stoke conversation between us, but that failed. Once the singing was over we had nothing to offer the Overseer, and from the beginning he had nothing to say to us. We ate his apples and grapes in silence. But the Reverend was not the kind to let opportunity slip by without plugging, and sometime before we left he had elicited a promise from the Overseer's wife that she would entertain one of his guilds early the coming year. The Reverend also had hoped that some unused company building might have been available for additional school space for the village, but the Overseer could make no promise about that. We left the comfortable, immaculate house and returned home in the dark.

He was a kind man, the Reverend. I hope wherever he is he learns nothing of what has become of me. I would not like him to feel in any way responsible. He taught me much — both purposely and unwittingly. For him I feel nothing but gratitude. Gratitude a little tainted, perhaps, but nevertheless gratitude. It is not my fault if I cannot forget his struggles with Betty. I have no control over my memory now, any more than I had control over the great disappointment I felt when on being taken into his charge I discovered things about him I never expected in a priest. The cigarettes beneath his cassock for instance, the rum secretly cached in his private cabinet. I had no control over my reaction to such things.

I am grateful to him for having taken an interest in my

education. His library was well stocked, and after our night of carolling at the Overseer's he gave me permission to use his books whenever I chose. 'Do you like reading, Marcus?' 'Yes sir.' 'Ever heard about King Arthur?' 'Oh yes, sir. He was king of the Round Table.' 'Wonderful legend. Here's the first volume . . .' 'Know anything about Shakespeare?' 'Oh yes, sir. I can recite To Be or Not To Be.' 'His sonnets? His plays?' 'What's a play, sir?' 'Here's a volume of his complete works . . .' 'Africa?' 'That's a bush country, sir.' 'Much more than that too. Ever heard of Johannesburg? Bloemfontein? Pretoria?' 'No, sir.' 'Wonderful book here . . .' And so it went. From adventure to adventure. From Merlin the magician to Cecil Rhodes the wizard, to the paralysed Hamlet, the confused Othello; Saracens and Richard Coeur de Lion; also Achilles, Hector, and Odysseus; Cleopatra; Genghis Kahn, Alexander; the Arabian genies; Erikson and Byrd; adventure piled on adventure, and every weekday between four and the Angelus my pulse danced and lunged with the conquest of these heroes or their valiant dying. In those days I too wanted to be a hero. Especially when on occasion the suspense and glory of some escapade came to me not from a book, but directly from the Reverend himself — from his parched, cracked lips that spun magic in so many different tongues. He had ridden sleds in Lapland, poled boats on the Volga, canoed up the Congo. Boars, elephants, lions, he had seen them all in the skin; and with his pink face glistening he could recreate dramas spellbinding enough to make my black skin pimple. Perhaps I was just an impressionable boy. In any case, those evenings at the Reverend's sprung my imagination so wide it never quite closed up again, and perhaps he would be pleased to learn this. Further, I am grateful to him for the other people I found in his library, those whom he never invited me to know but whom I nevertheless found. Above the shelves of adventure. These from the first appeared to be formidable volumes in sombre grey, or dull red jackets, and it was an unspoken understanding between the Reverend and myself that whatever wisdom these special covers guarded was not for me. But I took it. I remember well the first day I laid hands on Raynal. The old Abbé had things to say about slaves and slave-masters that I had read nowhere before, and his adventures did not take place in some distant land, but in the very archipelago where I was a native. Old Raynal was telling stories about my people. My great-grandparents, and their parents. About me. Here for the first time was a story saying that traders, settlers, and slavers were not necessarily heroic. John Hawkins and Walter Raleigh as villains were new. Who were the savages? Raynal's stories gave reason to that second nature fear and hatred I felt against the sons of the traders and slavers, their sons, nourishing their broad European behinds upon cruelties delivered against mine and me in the New World. That dusky evening, I remember sitting with the book on my knees long after the sexton had already rung the Angelus, my eyes bent low in the dark. I feared to stir lest I should call the Reverend's attention to my lingering presence in his library. He was in the next room. I could hear him. Even through Raynal's whippings, pillories, and bloodlettings I could hear the Reverend in the adjoining room . . . 'You are a pretty girl, Betty. Do you have a young man?' And the silence, when Betty must have put on her vacuous grin and let her head fall. That was her way. She was just three years older than I, smooth, milky black, with a face that never asked for anything it was so busy offering all she had — to men not boys. Most of the young men in the village, and some of the old ones too, knew Betty's special tree in the graveyard where those who dared run the gauntlet of ghosts could meet her and enjoy the sweetness for which she was so notorious. 'Do you have a young man?' Betty was servant at the vicarage. She cooked the Reverend's food, made his bed, and in his voice I could hear her being requested to perform additional services. 'Surely you have a young man who tells you how pretty you are, and touches you . . .' When everyone in the village knew that Betty was never short on touchings. 'You mustn't try to fool me. Don't you like little touchings?' 'No, sir.' Her voice just sufficiently more than a whisper to come through the wall. 'You mustn't try to fool me. I'm too experienced for that you know. Look at me.' Then a silence. 'Supper's almost ready, sir.' 'That can wait . . . Don't you like it?' Silence. 'Don't you like it? Your young man never touches you like that, does he?' Silence. 'I've seen so many girls like you along the Congo, along the Guinea Coast. How you stir up memories! Don't you like little touchings?' 'No.' Her voice still came discreetly. 'Stop. I say no.' The voice of a small but determined animal. And perhaps then she was looking the Reverend straight in the eye. Perhaps it was not so dark in the room he could not truly see her aversion. 'I'll have supper in fifteen minutes,' he said, and I knew it was time for me to return Raynal to his shelf.

Raynal, Hakluyt, Esquemeling, Hans Sloane, were all represented upon the Reverend-tutor's upper shelf, and as often as I dipped my nose into them he never once suspected. To my loss, perhaps, for he was a kind man and might have offered some guidance the way he did with my other reading. Without any guidance, why read past those chapters that bubbled blood? Much of great importance was probably missed through this style of reading, but I could never let him know of my intrusion. He had never quite said Raynal and company were restricted, but I felt convinced that had he found me with them I would have been forbidden the library altogether. And so I continued my furtive ways, reading and re-reading accounts of such and such a day through the Middle Passage; such and such a flogging, thumb-screwing, spurring, burning, waxing, hanging, gelding of such and such a master's slave; such and such a dealing with the Dahomey king; such and such a quelling of such and such a rebellion; but never once betraying the volcano of fear and protracted vengeance ready to erupt within me, while in between times with Betty the Reverend continued

64

to ply me with tales of his heroic adventures. He was a kind man. I am truly now a little sad that I felt compelled to be furtive with him, but that was all instinct. I could no more tell the Reverend-tutor that I had been disturbing his prize books than I could reveal having overheard him plead to get a hand beneath Betty's skirt, then into her drawers. How would he have taken it had I said to him, 'She's giving you a hard time because you're going about it all wrong.' Or the day when finally he got down on his knees, how would he have taken my saying, 'You're going about it all wrong. Make her get down on her knees.' And I would have been able to support this advice through citing a dozen young men who had been successful with her. Would he have taken it like a fellow friend? In any case, who knows what ecstacies he enjoyed down on his knees? That very day he told Betty she was his altar. It is well he was not denied making his profound supplication.

In the end Betty relented. And when she finally let down her trousers I had enough time to cart off the whole library was that my wish. Instead, I flicked on the electric light and stayed long after the early bats ceased whistling by outside the window. Eventually the tutor came in, redder than usual, and asked offhandedly, 'Are you still here reading?' Betty was by then rattling supper things in the kitchen, and singing too — a vulgar song. I pretended not to have realized what time it was, and he said, 'Run along now. Can't swallow it all in one day, you know.'

So the scheme became established. Betty with the Reverend-tutor, and I with his books.

But why go on? A detailed history of my days under the tutor is irrelevant. Suffice it to say I owe him much, and have always felt a deep gratitude for the many kindnesses he showed me. The day he packed his scarred wooden trunks and fastened the broad leather straps around them preparatory to departing our village, I did not want to see him go. It had been far easier parting with my own father. And whether my sorrow was really for the books already on their way to the steamer, and not for the man himself, it makes little difference. In those days I saw the man and his books as inseparable. I cried. For the Reverend-tutor had brought many new discoveries into my life and it seemed the days ahead without him must necessarily be quite empty. Further, there was much between us that remained unfinished. At the back of my mind I had hoped one day to bare my hatred, my thirst for vengeance against himself and others descended from those European slave-masters, and ask his help in deciding what to do about it. But after he left, the blood of his books continued in my dreams, and the fulminating desire to revenge my forebears gradually solidified into a burden. I hope the Reverend-tutor wherever he might be never finds out the end to which I am come. Generous as he is, he might take much of my guilt upon himself, and that would be unfair. My volcano had its beginnings long before I ever met him. He and his books only served, perhaps, to ripen it faster.

In the early days, when I ran the field a barefoot boy with my shirt-tail hanging, the white man was a face that passed its own judgements, behaved as it pleased; a face to be dreaded because it carried the magical power to paralyse and kill. In time that face passed. It had to — particularly after my acquaintance with the Reverend-tutor. So in my fifteenth year I had a revelation. Redface was a killer face, was also a wise face, kind, even generous sometimes, and not above weakness. Definitely not above being fooled. Always available to be fooled. The Reverend-tutor never knew the extent of the education I got in his library; neither did he know why Betty's young men laughed as he passed stepping spritely through the village. I laughed too when I was among them, for many were the dusks when soon after the last vibrations of the Angelus I heard him scream out his sperm, while never a sound came from Betty. And if he answered our laughter with a smile of his own, or if he stopped to talk cricket, then in going away politely remind me that I needed

66

some more time with my reading, that was only further proof that the face was far from all-seeing, and this reduced the dread somewhat.

The revelation of my fifteenth year did not so much banish the earlier definition of the white man, as supplement it. So I could fear, hate, distrust, admire him, and be affectionate towards him all at the same time. I could want to follow in his footsteps, see the things he had seen, travel the world and have adventures such as he had had. Though not precisely. I did not yearn to see Greenland, nor the Volga valley, nor China's great wall. Instead the jungle back of the Guinea Coast loomed tall in my dreams. The jungle and the Guinea Coast, bush huts, fires, and bloody compounds; the veldt between Bloemfontein and Pretoria where part of me once was a naked Kaffir fearless and deadly with my charmed assegai; the Middle Passage where chained on my back in the dark stink hold I was number one hundred and thirty-three, therefore number one to be saved from being dropped in the weed when brave Captain Colinwood sought to protect his owners against dead liabilities; Amsterdam, Cadiz, Liverpool, Marseilles, in each place my sweat and blood had been left behind in barracoons and monuments and private fortunes. I longed to travel in these places. I longed to make again that journey through the Middle Passage. Did I really survive such horrors? And the jungle — did I really suck out the brains of an uncle? Did I really cut teeth on the roasted testicles of some captured chieftain? And those ships, those dark stinking ships with shit pee vomit ever freshening on the irons, did I really come through all that? How incredible. And the white trader top-side, did he really take my sweat and blood back to London, Madrid, Paris, Lisbon, through the Zuider Zee in the shape of riches? The Indians, poor bastards, they had to mine the gold. But for me, poorer bastard, it was the field. Day after day. The clambake soil in July, the thick black mud in December. Always the field. And was it true? Did my suffering and decay really glitter like the Indian's gold? I mean, all the sugar, cocoa, coffee, bananas, and tobacco, did they turn the trick in Europe and really make somebody rich? Is it true that others have seen my death paraded with great pomp and finery in society, at court? And how did they distribute me? How much, what monuments exactly stand upon me in each place? I longed to find out. That's one thing the tutor's books did for me. They made me conscious of the sea as a connection. A connection between the several stages and states of myself that were scattered about the world. Not about the world exactly, but scattered in more or less of a triangle from West Africa to Europe to America. I longed to gather up these various deposits of myself — for I was but a shadow without them — and the sea was the only avenue. Until I could sail its blue-grey lanes on my own odyssey I was destined to remain a shadow in the New World; albeit one denied the airiness and freedom of shadows because of the great burden of unaccomplished vengeance growing heavier behind my chest each day.

Apostil

It should be remembered that Shepard's self-portrait, like most, will inevitably misrepresent the true story at certain points. Ego comfort? Myopia? Who knows what drives people to falsify in telling the story of their lives? So far, Marcus has not been perfect in at least two instances. On the subject of kites, Marcus claims that as a boy he never had pretty ones, seldom had any at all. Yet, among the villagers with whom he grew up he is remembered as a one-time fancy kite maker. As a former school companion tells it, 'Marcus? He a master when it come to making kites. Used to keep him a shoemaker's knife — nobody knows where he got it — so sharp, he could whittle box wood down to almost thin as paper itself. I remember, 'cause one time he chased me with that knife. Had him a temper, whew! But nobody touch him when it come to making kites. He'd get that wood whittled down thin, and put him some joints like a master joiner on that frame. If there wasn't no box wood, he'd get him some cocoyea from a dry coconut branch and put together a frame better than most people do with box wood. And design, whew! He make me a kite one time shape like a big heart. Circle in the centre of the heart, and outside that a star. Six point. That was the prettiest kite I ever had. When Marcus got through threading a design for you, didn't make any difference how the colours went.' Did he have kites of his own? 'Hell, most of the time people'd be giving him wood and paper, even money sometimes to buy his own, but he'd always say "Nah, man. Go

ahead. Just give me enough (whatever it was) to make your own".
This one villager could give no reason for Marcus' refusals. Many
people in a poor village like this would practise a folksy generosity,
but he is to this day convinced that Marcus never was a generous
person.

'Used to make kites for them white boys all the time,' another
villager tells. 'Never had time for people like me.'

'You're a damn liar,' says the first. 'Nobody ain't saying he
didn't make kites for them white boys but any time one of us wanted
a kite — or anything else — Marcus never said "No".'

'Ah, gwan! You be just like him if you had the chance — always
up under white people ass hole'!

'You say that 'bout me?'

'Yes, ah say that 'bout you.'

And they came to blows.

There was no conflict among the villagers in respect to Marcus'
attitude towards Betty and the Reverend. They all agreed Marcus
was naïve and didn't understand that the village approved Betty's
serving the bachelor priest. 'Well, her reputation was spoiled any
way,' one woman explained, 'and priest or no priest them bachelor
white men — some married ones too — all take advantage of our
young girls whenever they get the chance. Betty saved some of us
from having to get in bed with that one.' Was Betty sacrificed? In a
way, is the answer. Though a quick thinking young man points out
that it was really the priest who was sacrificed. 'That girl! I
don't believe that priest had to ask her for nothing. She had itchy-
bitchy and I believe she stayed on him day and night. He had to
run from the village in the end, and everybody know that why he
left. By the time he gone though, Betty's ready to settle down. Man,
if it wasn't him it might a been me getting racked out with her.'
Why not Marcus? The villagers laugh. Not hardly. His father had
been the one to break in Betty, and the girl had ever after felt very
motherly towards Marcus. It seems Marcus' father had been
quite notorious for breaking in young virgins. That's what led to
his having to run from home. An outraged Indian father had

70

ambushed him twice in attempts to cut off his penis. After the hair's breadth escape of the second time, with the Indian vowing to chop off whatever he could when next he was within arm's length of Marcus' father, the cocksman didn't wait around for a third encounter. Perhaps there was some connection between the Indian father and the redfaces — as Marcus calls them — but if so, it is not easily discovered.

It is remarkable that although Marcus in his youth had a full and eventful life among his village companions he barely mentions them so far in his story. Neither does he give us a full picture of the priest, whose departure is remembered quite clearly by many villagers. They recall that the priest had grown fat. The flesh at the back of his neck rolled over his collar, and his face had come to resemble a ripe papaya. Nobody knows why he had gotten so fat, or why his skin had turned from red to yellow. And though his congregation had dwindled away, many people turned out the day he left. He sat in the back seat of the motorcar with hands clasped on his stomach, and never once turned his yellow eyes on the crowd gathered before the vicarage. Not even to say goodbye to Marcus who was standing in front of everybody else crying like an infant. And as the car pulled off down the main road Marcus ran behind it crying something — 'Father' 'Come back' There is disagreement here — and everyone felt ashamed.

All of the villagers who knew Marcus remember his violent temper. The man whom he had chased with his knife recalls that Marcus at times trembled and cried when he was in a fit and couldn't find someone his size to hurt. Even The Undertaker — whom Marcus mentions — testified during the trial that Marcus was extremely short-tempered and violent. He said Marcus was mad; but that might have been an exaggeration.

How shall I walk? How shall I walk in this world — or in any other for that matter? What shall I do with my eyes? Shall I turn them inwards? Heaven knows they've been turned inward for quite a long time — not fully. We've also had to maintain an alert against dangers on the outside. Enough of a long time. Perhaps there might have been peace in being a crab with eyes on poles retractable, plastic enough to peer around corners, dispel beforehand the dangers that lurk along every road. But do crabs ever see on the inside?

July 9, 1952 — Wednesday

Enough of looking on the inside! Today I am a criminal. They were very careful not to use that word or otherwise call me names when they let me out of the jail on Monday. 'You can go, Shepard,' the Inspector said, though his voice promised the matter was far from closed. The promise was in his eye too that he would see me back behind bars, and more, before long. 'You can go, Shepard,' and I was free to walk out, take my place in the steamy streets of Port-of-Spain. They tried some at concealing their intentions for my future, but I am a criminal, I know; and as far as that goes, a truly free man. And that, most of all, was what they tried to cover — that room for freedom which every criminal must sense once it's established he roams outside the laws, outside the institutions which pillar and are pillared by the laws of the land or whatever. They were not quite ready, the Inspector, his lieutenants, the policemen, the judge, the witnesses, and they had to let me go. Their law. 'You can go now, Shepard' — and live your few remaining days in fear of what we have in store for you.

I know the Inspector's game. Already I see him, sooner or later, screaming up to my house in his little black car with the blue light flashing, marching in with his chest stuck out like some military bird, the final warrant in his hairy fingers. There was no goodbye between us. He had more days of painstaking investigation before him. He would order his policemen to question this person and that, might even journey to the village himself to question Grandfather and others there who know me. He would spend long hours in the spotless bungalow with Anthony's father, assuring the red-necked Overseer that justice would definitely take its course in the matter of his son's death. Near-sighted police clerks at Headquarters would receive hundreds of reports which they would copy and pass on to other clerks whose job it would be to bind the thick files on my case. And after that, after all the questioning, and reporting, and binding, the Inspector would take many cups of tea while poring over the files at night, organizing his prosecution. Then one morning, or midnight maybe, depending on how dramatic he wished to be — this little harbinger of doom — comes the little black car, siren and blue light going. I could have saved him all that trouble. I could have told him I was already prepared, and his dramatics would consequently be pointless — except as a ritual he ought to keep to himself. 'You can go, Shepard,' and as he announced my release I felt sorry for the sore feet his officers would suffer, ashamed for the fear that would strike Grandfather and his neighbours when the uniformed investigators knocked on their door. My impulse was to have a man to man talk with the Inspector, and explain everything to him. But he was very pompous in asking me to be quiet. 'We'll ask for your testimony when we need it.' A regular master official. Khaki uniform and puttees, and a full commitment to the routine of his duty. 'You can go, Shepard,' and I smiled at his stern eye, his commanding voice, because with all his frigid threatening he is into a flat fall, and all the evidence he compiles cannot put him together again. I am a criminal for the moment without a crime. Free. And, poor fellow, he has the task of tying me up to a crime, with motive, opportunity, and all the other things that have to be tied up before a judge may say GUILTY. And it would not have mattered had they never let me out of their jail. It was not an unpleasant place. They had me in a thick-walled cell, sub-surface, where it was cool, silent. Never before had I been in a place so continuously cool — almost cold — as my cell. And the silence? That was the best part of all. The silence. I saw no one, heard no one, other than the police servant and guard who brought me food once a day. It was peaceful. Pleasant and peaceful. Familiar too, as though a shade from childhood memory, or dream, had finally come to life. I was not unhappy in my cell. I would have been pleased to stay there for a long time.

It was quite a shock when they put me out. 'You can leave, Shepard,' and, next thing, the shocking light of a day brighter than any I've ever seen. The sun was almost white, and my eyes, at first refusing to face it, blinked and fluttered and threatened to remain closed forever. I forced them open. I had to walk. And even though the Inspector had made me a free man, I didn't know how to walk without my eyes. This new daylight was everywhere. The sky, the roofs, even the rusty-brown walls and gate of the jail, as I looked back, were covered in this shimmering white-gold light. And the clouds too, low clouds sailing in over the northern hills bringing their afternoon rain, they were sheathed in the sharp light too, so that they came like incandescent balls, grey and bilious at the core, with fluffy edges that seemed to be laughing, or snarling, whichever rainclouds do. I went back to the prison gates, but they were locked and I couldn't get in. I rattled the great chain in the hopes that some guard would come to check the disturbance and I could then send to the Inspector saying I wanted to return to my cell. But no one came. They probably had a laugh behind their windows; laugh at the crazy fool who thought he could shake himself up some attention at the gates of their jail. I turned away again, and went on. There wasn't much to do. I wandered through several streets, or so it seemed; although a certain corner came to seem familiar, as though I might have gone around the jail more than once. I'm not sure. But it was a quiet neighbour-hood. The neighbourhood in which our best citizens live. The houses are tall and clean, with hanging verandahs enclosed by wrought iron banisters. The yards are clean and well carved too — what one could see of them. For they are enclosed on every side by brick or hibiscus fences, each with its wrought iron gate properly chained and locked. Purely accident, I am sure, but our jail stands in the middle of our best neighbourhood, and is itself the finest of the fine residences. The others, with all their well-trimmed fences, open galleries, and concrete pathways, are little replicas of the real thing. The jail remains the epitome of elegance and peace in our best neighbourhood, and it was with a little feeling of sadness that I finally turned away from there and wandered to the city square.

Wasn't much to do there either, except stay out of the way of the hurrying midday crowds, and wait for the afternoon shower to relieve the heat. I stretched out on an empty bench beneath a tree, and closed my eyes to rest them from the fierce light. When I managed to shut out the voices and footsteps of the shoppers and lunch lazy clerks, the rumble and blare of motorcars, and all the other jangle of town machinery, it was quiet. Quiet as it must have been before Columbus came, and my thoughts drifted back to that time when the Caribs must have, their fishing done, awaited the afternoon showers in peace. Back to the time when there was no Port-of-Spain; when what became Port-of-Spain must have been a broad mangrove swamp in which the Caribs set traps for the Arawaks. A time of peace, yes, except when the Arawaks came woman

75

hunting. Any slight noise in the midday stillness then must have made the heart flutter; and that must have been a terrible noise itself — heart fluttering. But no two Indian tribes, fierce as they might be, ever shook really the languid stillness of a tropical midday. What tree ever deigned to shake a leaf even though the thunder of a chief going down under his enemy's stone buffeted and echoed up to the hills? The people, braves and cowards, the dying and the killers, they must have paused though, and in a second felt each his soul stirred by that awful thunder, that noise of things we would have endless coming to a still end.

In the village Thunder was unmatched for raising fear in young and old alike. When he bellowed just before dawn each day everyone knew what was happening, and every head, startled or awake, burrowed deeper beneath the covers because you couldn't lose your soul if you didn't see. And the dare was in Thunder's resplendent face shining down over the whole village at that hour of the morning. They taught me early never to look up at lightning, or if it came upon me unexpectedly to close my eyes. It will blind you, they said. You will lose your soul to Satan, they said. And I was afraid. We had examples too in the village of those who had been careless or wilful. There was Iva, who sat all day in the shade of the rumshop eave peeing on herself. And Berry, he couldn't wink any more. When he slept propped up between the pickle barrel and sticky damp sugar sacks flies laid eggs on his pupils. And there was Grandee who walked with a limp, but who was so fierce, and could throw his stick so hard we had to tease him from afar. And my father, some people said, belonged to the devil too: that's why he had such a beautiful singing voice, such a charming singing voice, and young girls were warned against listening to him. Young girls, and grown women too. They warned each other. And I was expected to follow in his footsteps, especially as I had a decent choir voice. Is it true he listened too much to Thunder? I always tried to close my ears because there was something in Thunder's voice that made me want to see him — and I never believed I could do that without paying some terrible price. The tutor said it was all superstition and nonsense. He said so. Until I had heard him often enough to begin thinking maybe, and finally I went to see Thunder myself.

Midday. I did not believe the priest soundly enough to go when it was dark. Midday, after I had hidden from Paul and Len and Bob on our way back to school, and they gave up trampling through the hedges, gave up chucking rocks into the trees through which we played and went on without me. They thought I had fooled them and gone ahead, but I had fooled them and stayed behind, until I couldn't hear them any more. Then I set off for the dairy. I went through the burnt fields, and my clothes picked up a lot of black soot for which I knew I would be whipped. But we had all watched the fire three nights before, watched the mongoose and manicou and some snakes come racing from the blaze, and we had chased whichever we pleased, except the snakes, because they were most of the time too hard to find. And next day we had watched the cane-cutters, their blades flashing rhythmically above their heads, and the women loaders who bound the cane into bundles then loaded the carts, and the mule-drivers, kings of the fields, who had beautiful voices that did not come on the air, just sprang from it. I knew the fields. I had been in them every year before, and I knew they would get my clothes black, but I still tried being very careful and that helped to make a good adventure. On my way across the empty fields to see Thunder, the terror of our village, the devil's spokesman. And when I came to the dairy I circled far from the dairyman's whitewashed house, the cluster of barns and outside buildings, staying always to the empty fields, until I approached the wired-in pasture where everybody knew Thunder grazed. It was a very big adventure, being alone in the fields at midday. There was no shade, not even where the wired-in pasture humped over into the gully through which I came.

I have seen that. Shade where fields hump over into one another; but there was none this day. I waited at the fence. It would have been a better adventure to climb the fence and search for Thunder inside his own pasture, but I didn't do that. I might have, if I could have seen over the hump of the pasture, but I wasn't tall enough for that so I squatted in the gully with my back to the sun, waiting. Then after a while I sat down; because I had the whole afternoon: tropic afternoon, drowsy once you sat down, silent, except for the flies and bees humming in steady subterranean voice that undermined the whole silence. Mass-like hypnotism. I didn't mean to give in; I didn't mean to let the silence penetrate so far that I could join it in doze, but I did. And when for some reason my eyes fluttered open, I saw Thunder staring at me. He looked very ordinary. Nothing but a broad black bull with short in-curved horns, and three or four inches of drool hanging from his nose. He looked very ordinary, even when he shivered his skin to scatter a minor cloud of flies. Then I fell on to Thunder's eyes, and couldn't get away. Only once before had I seen such eyes. Once when gravedigger Samuel was drunk on the rumshop floor with flies buzzing inside his mouth and nose, his red eyes had the Devil looking through them. I got to my feet and scrambled a little left, away from the fence. Thunder's head followed, stopping when I stopped. I ran to the right and the same thing happened. Then I chucked lumps of dried dirt at him, lumps that scattered into sand long before they fell at his feet, but I dared not take my eyes away to look for solid pieces. Our eyes were locked; it was disaster for the one to let go. At the same time, a fight against being paralysed. Paralysis accumulated through the many pre-dawn shivers, fright swelling, swelling. Thunder broke. In a rapid charge of hot air, hotter than the day itself, which I felt, felt and heard coming, first a mere grumble down inside the broad black body, running into a raw rumble, exploding every corner of the silence, a terrific liquid blast, remote yet so near there was nothing more to hear until it funnelled into an upturned shriek hysterically cornering down even though Thunder's head remained upturned, pointing at the sky. Run! Thunder bellowed, run! There was nothing to do but run, after feeling that thunderous bellow. Run, making a little noise myself somewhere between a sniffle and a sob, which nevertheless was heard loudly in my own ear, then I was ashamed for having lost courage.

Run across the broken fields, with the back of my neck still fanned by that strange hot breath, but my neck on the whole stiff from being afraid to look around. Mingled shame and vows of vengeance, shame and fright and childish vows of vengeance clouding my eyes even up to the crest of the field more than quarter mile away, where yet I still couldn't see well for the clouds in my eye, still couldn't look back; for no matter what my mind said, in other parts I knew being chased with a hot breath, knew too that the demon lurking upon my neck could have no victory as long as I saved my eyes. Where shall I put my eyes? Run, even unto the Reverend-tutor, who had some advice: 'Rot, pure rot, my boy. I've been all over the world, but I've yet to meet a bunch more superstitious than this one here. And there's really no need for it; no need at all. Thunder's merely an animal. I've seen him myself. A dumb four-legged animal, fenced in at that. Couldn't possibly have broken out of his field, and chased you all the way here, could he? Look, there's a new Priestley just come. Read it and take your mind off that silly black animal.'

So, set my eyes into *The City of Gold* for the time being, among Kaffirs, Boers, civilized guns and savage assegais; bodies and a lot of blood between Pretoria and Bloemfontein. Kraals upon a diamond site into red flames, blazing forge glory, and the city of gold. Adventure in the breeches of Cecil Rhodes. In his brain, his heel too. Not enough. Not really the right thing either. So after a while Betty came back from wherever she had been spending the day. The muttering voices, preparations for the naked tussle in the Reverend's bedroom. Started. And it was safe then to put the cover down on Priestley and open Bunyan instead. Christian, he was really a hero. Bantu war cries were frightening, but not half so frightening as the valley through which Christian must pass, and he did it every time. I read him over and over, navigating between pitfalls and treacheries. During about the fifth reading came please-aaah, don't-oooh! A plunging frenzy brave Christian; twisted, remote from every paradise, yet not so twisting nor remote as the demon voice standing on its last note through the dusk. Oh save us from the perils of this day; perils, paralysis not the least. Reverend-tutor so right. Of course I did not want to outface a miserable black bull. Keep your eyes upon the citadel of gold, shining, shimmering, golden-milky in the distance; white, pure white, at a great distance; visible and alluring, always. So there shall I keep my eyes, always upon the pure white-in-the-distance, knowing, understanding that the golden-milky was just a mere sheath over the furious black core. Cores of flame. Black red. Keep my eyes; if only I could silence that voice in my blood, 'Eyes down: What're you looking at, boy?' Silence it. Stop it from getting louder. Stop it from getting so damn loud you could hear no other — 'EYES DOWN! WHAT THE HELL YOU LOOKING AT, BOY?' So loud, it barely does not shatter you to bits. Blood voices on the inside, thunder bellows on the outside, and in the distance a golden citadel jarred and blurry, but ever there, shimmering, alluring . . .

The rain came down, and stretched out on the bench I let the warm drops blat my face a little before I sat up.

So one day soon the Inspector will come, and I must be prepared to face him. No show. Not the least show.

The raindrops were very broad, and my shirt was soaked all the way through before I made it to the shelter of a better tree. By then, shelter didn't matter. I wandered out into the street, and for the first time in my life found pleasure in the rain. Do all criminals find pleasure in the rain? The drops came loud, slashing off my head and neck, stinging momentary clusters of soft pain along my scalp and skin. And as if that were not enough, the ricochet and rhythm, sending delayed rivulets down my neck, my spine, raising more hell down that path than Hille has ever been able to, try her hardest. I must have looked a fool to the shelterers. They certainly looked a bunch of fools to me — the shoppers, idlers, vagrants, what-have-yous, crammed belly to backside beneath the narrow eaves, wet anyway from the sweat that never stops, rain or no rain; the sweat each day would have, dawn to dark, and many times beyond on into near dawn, so that out of twenty-four hours maybe two or three would be dry. It took my time in jail to make me realise there was little difference between sweating and rain-wetting. The trick was to remain dry. And if that couldn't come to pass, then the thing to do was get all wet, completely wet, until the skin accepted wetness, enjoyed it. They looked a bunch of fools to me; cramped beneath the eaves, mopping at their faces with limp handkerchiefs. I went by one who was an innovator. He had himself a tree, one of those trees that draw food from God knows where in a city, obviously spared, but bold, defiant enough to buckle the sidewalk with its underground contortions. He, pressed against the rough-barked trunk, had himself a tree. His eyes said of me very loudly, 'fool', then as I met them, 'crazy?' and I thought, yeah! Thunder voices, lightning streaks; trees are not such dumb avengers, after all. Then as suddenly as it had lashed out from the sky the rain withdrew, and I found my feet had the meanwhile taken me to George Street.

George Street named after a monarch was not the same. That yellow-white light. Coming back, once the grey rainclouds were finished, had passed away. Look up. Telephone wires strung slackly like strings on a tired guitar, sagging fret to fret across a box still dazzling white. What tunes who played? My father sang each Saturday night. Even after he disappeared we heard from visitors and other village wanderers how his high silk voice still charmed the females so, he never suffered want of food or any of the other things females provide. Mother rarely sang, and, always, when she thought she was not being over-heard. I doubt she ever learned a single song completely, tune or lyrics. Dum di di dee da dum in an off-key voice was usually how she said it to herself, and I didn't dare help or correct her, lyrics or tune, because then she would shut up completely. And I didn't dare correct father either, who mispronounced the lyrics sometimes, flatted or sharped in the wrong places some-times, because there was no fury like that with which he could say, 'I been singing that song long before any half dumb fool put words to it. Just because there's a war every clown's taking up songwriting. What the hell do they know about songwriting? Flatting and sharping in the wrong places purposely he would go on, leaving me behind with the feeling I had been in error where there obviously was no error possible. But my mother was the only woman we knew who did not love him for his singing voice. So that when stories came Grandfather and I at the beginning were always sure of the ending, and waited for it to come close enough for him to shout, 'What're you doing in this room, boy? Get out.' But that never prevented me from listening outside the door, or window. And it always ended the same, whether the teller was an old village friend, or a stranger just passing through — 'You have one hell of a boy, Pappa Jay' even though my father was never a boy that I could remember. 'You have one hell of a boy. Before Maynard's back turned good your boy had her ass in his hands, and there ain't nothing now she won't do for him. Maynard knows it too — or knows about it, anyway. But I ain't ever seen nobody as slippery as your boy ... ' Always the same whether the teller was an old acquaintance or a stranger just passing through, because by this time the tall square bottle of rum would be down low. And I could always tell by the silence that followed the voice, and the two spatterings of liquid — rum, bare back; everybody drinks grog straight in the presence of Pappa Jay — into the drinking glasses, I could always tell almost down to the second when

Grandfather would bawl, 'Boy!' And I would have to wait as though I were coming from the bottom of the yard before I answered, breathless. And the change from the store that day would be mine, nor would Grandfather notice if the rum was an inch lower than it ought to have been, nor would he test to see if water had been added. Then one day he said to me I shouldn't believe everything storytellers tell, because quite often they didn't know what they were talking about. Then, another day, after a fresh story came, Grandfather didn't call for me at all, and I was glad, because I wouldn't have been able to answer if he had called. That day the story didn't end the same, and that made everything different. Grandfather didn't bawl 'Boy!', no noisy trickle of rum into the drinking glasses, nothing. It felt, from where I crouched outside the door, as though everything had come to a stop in there, even the breathing. And I have wondered since whether the story-teller of such a tale spent ever after a waking day without the tears — remembering or feeling them perhaps even tasting them — for that's what was happening in the long silence, only I didn't know it until later; Grandfather hunched over his rocker, staring out the window with his dim red animal eyes saying nothing except two full trickles separately down the black wrinkled-leather face; plop down into his crotch. I couldn't know it, because stooped listening outside the door I made my own trickles, without so much as ever once bursting into that room and telling the story-teller to keep talking. I wanted to too. I wanted to very much. Just to burst in there and say, 'Keep talking. What you mean ending the story like that? That's MY father . . . ' But I didn't. I just slumped to the floor in the hallway and made trickles. Don't even remember where they fell — if they fell. Think what happened was I wiped them away. And after a while, when Grandfather still said nothing, the story-teller opened the door, came out, passed out of our house. He left, but he knew what he was talking about, so his story remained and we couldn't change the ending.

I never did find out for sure why Grandfather cried. I know

now — I can admit now — why I did. I felt cheated. Felt left out, left behind. And that was not the first time. There he was, the old man hunched over like a parched monkey togged out in worn khakis all done up, even the patch edges pressed smooth and shiny, his liquid red eyes fixed out the open window. He was there — had always been there, it seemed, and I couldn't think of a time when he wouldn't be — but he was not enough. He was not enough to hold me still and stop the trembling, disappear that vacuum down which I lurched, nor fill it with sweet light. Father was dead.

That was years, many years it seems like, after that time when I stumbled away from Thunder, blubbering across the fields for a whole afternoon to see. But it was the same year in which I had earlier cried exactly for being left behind again, and Grandfather had been there too, only in that earlier time he didn't cry himself, he swore. Because for me he had set forth a wish, his wish, and I to be the fulfilment. And it was in the pursuance of this fulfilment that I found myself, after my dozen eggs broken in the field, after countless lengths of the strap against my back for interfering with this and that which definitely held no concern for little black boys who must walk the true hard path, after many fistfuls of sand in the eye and years of barked shins against the hot pitch-walks, and those never to be forgotten days in the study of the tutor, I found myself a student at the town high school. And I would not have been there except for Grandfather who had by this time closed his doors to all females and retreated into the depths of his weathered, lopsided house where mine were the only other feet he tolerated. I, he was determined, would have the opportunity to write a book of truth, the likes of which he would himself have written had he not been forced to spend so many of his years labouring in the fields, and were he wiser than to have spent so many others chasing his hands beneath the skirts of various women. 'The boy must have an education,' he said, and by this, it turned out, he meant something far different from what we discovered at the high school. The high school meant Latin and Shakespeare, and Pope and Bacon and Geometry, Algebra, Geography, and foreign languages and histories. Grandfather had meant most of these too — all of them, really — except, particularly with languages and histories, he found them too white. 'Nothing but murder and revenge, theft and counter-theft. That's all,' he said. 'Don't believe a damn all this fart about honour and glory, do you hear me!' That's what he said. 'Honour and glory! Let them tell about the other side in the Crusades. Let them tell that story too.' And, yes, I had to defend my textbooks — a simple matter where the Crusades were concerned. We were Christians, they were barbarians. 'Get OUT OF MY SIGHT! GET OUT! Is this what I pay money for? To have you talk like a damn fool? Get Out!' And on foreign languages, they were all right except he couldn't see the need for all this Latin and French and Spanish and German when all a man needed to know was his own tongue: and nobody was teaching Yoruba. What the hell anybody wanted to talk like Germans for, anyway? There was only one language a man needed to know if he couldn't get his own, and that was the good, real, ancient, old-time Hebrew. That good old Hebrew which alone could tell a man the secrets he needed to know; secrets dating back to that time when there were no foreign languages. And I didn't open my mouth to defend the texts this time because in my bones I sort of believed outright Grandfather was right about those secrets. For if I could discover what then seemed quite a few, now only one or two, in common English in the tutor's library, what must there not be waiting trapped in the first language? I didn't open my mouth to defend those texts, and we then had a peacemaking time before he blew out the lamp and we went to sleep.

'Marcus, get me a nip before you go to school.' So our days would begin. And when it was time for me to wheel my new bicycle out of the house and pedal an envious trail through village friends, on to school in the town, there he would be positioned in the rocker beneath his window — never closed except for rain — the uncorked bottle in one hand, his Bible opened in the other. How long he sat like that? All day, perhaps; for when I came home in the late afternoon he would still be in the same position — a gnarled old man, with sweat coursing through the crevices in his prune-wrinkled face, the circular tuft of hair around his temples sticking up like damp wool, his red eyes intent upon the Bible, the empty bottle beside his chair. It occurs to me now I have never seen Grandfather's eyes any other colour. What sights had they seen to make them so perpetually red — a liquid red that seemed a dead end bog of some stream stretching far back into his brain?

STUPID! Remember, not the least show. Be calm. Not the least show.

It is known that no man spends a lifetime in the tropics without having his eyeballs burned red. No man spends his lifetime in the tropical sugar-cane fields without having his eyeballs burned red in the wake of dust from the cracked earth, cane pollen, salty sweat streaks, sunlight so abrasive after every wink. Red eyes an inevitability.

And after I had carefully dusted my bicycle and rolled it into place beside my bed he would call, 'Marcus, boy, come and read to me from Solomon.' Sometimes, with his head resting against the tall back of the chair he would doze, puffing a rum stink snore into the room. But always should I stop, he would awake, quite cogent, saying, 'That's enough from the Bible. Where is your history book?' And I would read to him from that. Read to him of kings and queens not quite as wise as Solomon and Sheba, and therefore far more susceptible to his contempt. Richard, Elizabeth, Mary and Victoria and Edward and George, he would stop me to explain how wicked they were in spirit, even though the book never said so, even though the book praised their names after a fashion. An exhortation full and violent. 'The meek shall inherit the earth.' 'Blessed are the pure in heart.'

And I would be asked to read from some other book — Geography, or Shakespeare, it didn't matter which, so he could stop me at will saying, 'You're learning how to read and write, and someday you're going to get the chance I missed, the chance to write a book that tells the truth. I'll be dead and gone, but remember what I say. You can't write the truth if you don't see it. A man's got to see first. Learn what these school books say, but don't let that blind you ... ' I never understood in those days, perhaps still don't, what he meant by truth. At the jail I did discover that many of the things I knew or seemed to know began and ended right there inside me, and, I suppose, if I could ever make that inside knowing known on the outside, that would be a truth. Like with Anthony. If I had understood what Grandfather was talking about in those days, perhaps I never would have come to think of Anthony and myself as special friends. That is, I would have continued to think that we were special friends, but in a different way — he a special friend to me, I a special friend to him; not both of us special friends. And, we were like that — he a special friend to me, I a special friend to him — my acquaintance of the kite day and I. We rode our bicycles side by side from our village to town, and for all the other boys — black, red, or otherwise — who roamed the high school grounds we were 'the country boys'. It became a common thing for them on Fridays to puncture our tyres and trap us afoot — especially the red boys for whom Anthony was a debased version of themselves. Trap us afoot for their own sport. So after a while we got smart and commenced to hide our bicycles on Friday mornings. And the afternoons when the town boys massed at certain corners to pelt us with lumps of dirt and rotting lemons, we took turns drawing the fire. Anthony could sprint. He could really raise hell on that bicycle. Many Fridays when it was his turn to go before I saw nothing but his behind cocked in the wind for perhaps half the distance to our village; and then after I caught up it would be a race in dead earnest. What a sight we must have been — shirt-tails flying, legs pumping, our heads rigid set like horses! And for ten or twelve minutes there would be nothing else in the world but trees and houses passing backwards on the sidelines, sometimes an old woman, old man in the ankle high grass. Ting ting ting ... Whrrrrr ... Bike going good. Faster. Wait for the right time. The right time. Faster! BREAK! Through past the village shop where the idlers waited — idlers always waiting, to send up a noise. And if I were in front, a good noise. All cheering. If Anthony was in front, a bad noise — for every voice cheering him, three booing me. Nobody much liked to see Anthony win. And quarter mile from Pappa Jay's house it would come to an end. We would say nothing about racing, Anthony and I, but one rode ahead, the other dropped behind, saving any offence against Grandfather who forever warned me against Anthony as a riding or other companion.

In those days, too young to trust Grandfather's knowing, at the same time too young to disobey. I dropped behind or rode ahead for his sake: but always, once the race was done, one day Anthony and I would grow up, I believed, and carry that Friday spirit into a great world adventure. Not the racing so much — that was for the idlers, the watchers. But the sending before, the going behind, the scheming, the outwitting of whoever whatever town boys grew up into. This we would turn into a good adventure. And that would be all right, because by that time Grandfather would be gone, would not be — poor fellow — around to have to admit that he was wrong. So it was okay to appease him then, as long as he never found out that many nights when he thought I had gone to church, as I had left home to do, I was in fact crawling beneath the barbed wire surrounding Anthony's father's paradise. Old redface. He had a fence eight strands high, a dog, and a watchman. And Anthony never said it, but I understood his father said to him what Grandfather said to me — only in whatever way he had of talking to his son. Hence the crawling beneath the fence to a pre-arranged meeting in the shadow of the water tank, in the shadow of a bush, or tree, and

88

further crawling across the rest of an estate wide and graceful even in the dark, until we came to the servant's quarters and found her room. She, the sister of Betty, black and smooth, with the whitest teeth, the happiest eyes, and a bosom warm, softer than, more yielding than any I could imagine out of a pillow; smiling Cleo who always first looked surprised then pleased, and placing a finger to her pursed lips would tip backwards into the room swinging the door wider. 'You're going to have to stop coming if you can't make less noise.' While she squeezed the door to, then turned off the light. And, true, in the barrack next to Cleo was old Mammy Maude who had given birth to several half-white children herself in her time and was known as the best servant in all the quarters. But Mammy was the cook, and cooks work later hours than maids; so much breathing in the darkness then, until, 'Well, what you all come for?' 'Nothing.' 'Well, what you come for then?' 'To see you.' 'I've seen enough seeing all day. If that's all you come for you can go way and let me get my rest.' But no one moved. In time a rustling joins breathing, and then, 'Tony! You've been taking your father's money? Just today I hear him say to your mamma . . . ' 'It's my money.' And as I hear it now, there was a sadness in that voice. A sadness I was too young to recognize, but which Cleo might have sensed, might have wished to soothe by saying, 'I don't mean to say you're stealing . . . ' And Anthony, too young himself to know what he was feeling either — the sadness that later showed plain on his face, and made it hard for him to say anything at all, saying, even before he was ready sometimes, 'If they say anything to you about the money, I'll tell them I took it.' By then, seen in the dark, his face long and steady and serious, the hair half falling over the left side of his forehead. Cleo smiling then — I could tell, seeing the white half moon of teeth in the darkness — smiling, asking, 'And what you got?' 'Nothing.' 'You always got nothing. Don't your grandfather ever have any change round the house? That's one old man who's got to have something. How come . . . ' 'I didn't find it yet.' 'Well, when you find it don't forget to make up for all these times.' Smiling again in the dark, chuckling down behind her breasts, bare now, and just slightly less smooth than the dark, waiting. Anthony to his, and I to mine. She had hairs around one nipple, and I liked that one best. Anthony didn't seem to care. Except, he always managed to get his arm lower than mine around her waist; while Cleo chuckled and squirmed beneath our hands let free to go any place except beneath her petticoat — beneath her skirt, but not beneath her petticoat — while Cleo, chuckling, fondled our erections, one in each hand.

And in those days, I didn't trust Grandfather's knowing about love and women either. 'I'm free at last boy. I'm telling you I'm free. Not another female to put a foot in my door. And listen to me boy, don't let no female be your doom. You understand? Don't let no female be your doom. Their flesh is their flesh, and can't ever be yours.' While of course I didn't understand nor wished to understand. Grandfather had lost his last teeth. Whenever the meat was tough, I got it. What could he tell me about flesh? A dried up old man whose loins had gone dead? I couldn't trust his knowing because, when he said 'free' I heard 'dead', and I was too young for that. I longed to be swallowed up: to be lost forever snug in Cleo, to get deeply lost into her hot breath, her cupped hand, even while she insisted, 'You look under his pillow? Search his old clothes. Look in back of the mirror . . . ' But I had done all that — although if I had ever found Grandfather's savings I don't know what I would have done with them. 'It's got to be somewhere in the house,' saying, coming in a voice going cold, going distant, away from me. So hurriedly I would have to say, 'I saw him hiding something in a jar yesterday, but I didn't get a chance to look in it yet,' Growing cold myself abruptly, and trembling. Steeling myself, waiting to hear, 'Don't come back if . . . ' And though Cleo's voice never went away quite that far, there was no getting unsteeled or warm again. That's how bad nights ended. Other nights when I managed comic books or chocolate candy bars which she liked equally as well, there would be no fight against going away, and growing cold. Chuckles and fast breathing in the darkness, prickly skin hot between the thighs; and afterwards Anthony and I wandering off down to the pond, broad, snake-glistened in the moonlight. Always moonlight it seems, because when it was dark one felt and smelled the pond but did not see the unceasing riplets snaking whichever way the breeze blew. Still damp between the thighs, Anthony and I to make plans — first of all to see Cleo again, and then, as the pond breeze came rank in our nostrils, plans for the ultimate spiriting away to some place where we could have her all to ourselves. But this latter was more Anthony's plan than mine; for he could sit between the reeds above the bright pond and moon about the day when he would leave the tropical land for his true home across the water, complete with his books, bicycle, and Cleo smuggled somehow into his berth aboard the liner. More his plan than mine because I knew nothing of liners then (nor now) and that part of me that longed to cross the ocean was still too young, too timid, to be anything but resentful. I'll be revenged on you one day Anthony! A moment's cry — that moment again in which I lost my shirt and eggs. It filled my belly with a fire. I'll be revenged on you Anthony! Because Cleo, she likes new things. Lights up behind apples and chocolate bars, much more a trip across in an ocean liner. She'll go. Of course she'll go. She likes new things. Nothing newer than a liner. Charleston, Cadiz, Singapore, Macao, Liverpool, every one brand new too. With Anthony leading her around. It would have to be Anthony, because he was the one with people there. Everywhere for Anthony, liners and people. For me, ghosts. Even Anthony was a ghost. Kept shifting. In one moment, a fire in the belly blazing revenge; in the next, there we were, fast friends. A duo out to trick the world. Plans for Cleo and Cadiz; plans for our village too — its sprouting the omniscient grandeur necessary to the birthplace (that wasn't quite correct but we let it go) of twin heroes. Anthony from one side of the pond, I from the other. We were friends. In spite of Grandfather, redface, town boys, and perhaps Cleo, we were friends. Twin adventurers! Desert, tundra, jungle alike awaited our coming. And dreaming held myself together until that smouldering in the belly went away.

There was the night in December when Anthony and I at fifteen found ourselves in Cleo's room, but she was not the gay, teasing, friendly woman we knew. I knew. She seemed sultry and restless. And when we put our hands on her she glared like a wild horse considering, it seemed, whether to devour them in a single hot breath or not. By then I had developed plans for her, plans that had nothing to do with spiriting her away, but instead plans which simply readmitted me to her room after Anthony and I would have left together. He knew nothing of my plans, nor did she. And I was determined on that night I would bring back no staying-awake dreams and half-made erections to my room in Grandfather's house. I feigned ignorance of her peculiar mood and waited for the evening to run its regular pattern. I had it completely worked out. I would not spend much time with Anthony at the pond; and after I left him there to go home I would return to Cleo's window by an opposite trace. Anthony himself seemed a little solemn that night, but I was satisfied enough with myself not to pay much attention to him. Until out of her restlessness Cleo said, 'Sure would be nice to have some apples.' 'You had apples today,' Anthony said. 'Me?' Distressed. 'If your mama see me take so much as one of her apples she fires me!' There was a little silence in which I felt I should be saying something, but there was nothing for me to say — so I kept silent. Finally Anthony said, 'I'll get some apples,' and left the room. For a moment after he was gone I looked at Cleo, her nostrils flaring, her eyes averted. Then, sucking in a breath that would keep me for a long time, I put both arms around her. It was the same tight room with bed, bureau, and no chairs. The same low window that was always latched covered by a heavy print curtain, the

92

same high window in the opposite wall, narrower, uncovered, letting in a beam from the night light which shone perpetually from atop the big house. And Cleo. On the hard iron cot propped against two pillows, her legs tucked to one side. Rose talcum, incense, and a little whiff of sweat. Woman sweat. And her hot fast breathing in my ear, only none of it for me, her body said, where it shivered and stiffened beneath my hands.

In that tight room with its odours and no light, save a high streak through the smaller window, Cleo set both hands upon my shoulders, and before she said it I knew, even though the words came faster than I could move. And afterwards I didn't move. 'Don't come back,' she said. I didn't move, and she twisted herself free a little. 'After tonight you can't come back no more,' she said. 'Why?' Sounding small, weak, even though that was the last thing I wanted to be. 'Can't have you both at the same time no more,' she said. 'But I can still come. By myself.' 'No, you can't,' she said. 'Well how about Anthony?' 'He lives here. This his house.' 'I know it's his house. And he's my friend.' 'That white boy your friend?' 'Yes. He is my friend. Besides, I know how to come by myself. I want to come back tonight.' She laughed. 'That white boy your friend?' 'Yes. He is my friend.' She laughed again, and I had to let her go. 'Even if it was all right for you to keep on coming you couldn't come back tonight.' 'Why not?' 'Your friend's already coming back.'

I squirmed then. Had to sit away from her. And just as I was too young to trust Grandfather knowing about women and flesh, I was too young to understand clearly what Cleo was saying to me. In that moment when it became clear that all my careful planning was useless, I could neither think nor feel anything but how empty this night would be. Her smooth black face, her eyes and half moon teeth, the devouring mysteries I imagined covered beneath her petticoat, once shut off from me became the finest, bestest, onliest in the world, and I cried. But quietly. And not much. Partly because I had picked up somewhere the practice of holding myself together, partly because at that moment Anthony returned with a small paper sack of apples which he dumped on the bed as if to say, 'Spoils. You may feast.'

We ate.

I ate the tasteless apple listening to the crunch in my own ear. Cleo ate, and with her restlessness returned she snorted a little sharper, rolled her eyes a little wilder, but it was all for Anthony. And they had secret signs between them I was sure, for when he levelled his eyes upon her breasts she heaved higher and faster, and I was left out. I sat with my legs crossed and swallowed the tasteless apple, and although no one said a word I knew that I should get up and leave the room, but I was too weak for that sort of moving so I waited. And watched Anthony in the half light of the room in which his head glistened. Outline of a death's skull as I see it now. But then, not a death skull at all, glistening, smoothly curved where mine was broad, clean and sharp where mine was blunt. Never would he have to sit in a place where he wasn't wanted, pulling his insides together. And in the unknowing of that year I admired him, for he was a living example of all the heroes the tutor told about, and if I were to have any part of adventure at all it could never be done without him. Perhaps his aide. His servant? Both posts too small for me, and yet I was no rival; an empty rival who could but sit munching tasteless fruit, going bitter on the salt so vehemently swallowed back.

When the apples were finished Cleo wanted grapes. 'If I so much as smell them, your mama'd fire my tail from here to kingdom come . . . ' And tossing his hair back from his forehead Anthony lifted himself off the bed, marched through the door with his chest stuck out, a rocking sway to his shoulders. Swiftly, in the time it took me to think what could I say, he returned with another paper sack, dumped it more victoriously than the first, and we had grapes. Long, red, tough grapes that were sweet; even though none were offered me, and I had to

94

reach over Cleo's tucked in legs to help myself, all the while careful to keep my eyes away from the rest of her reclined among the pillows. And if I were Anthony sitting against her flank I would have been proud. She chewed the grapes noisily, sufficiently so to let everyone knew how sweet she found them. But I don't know if Anthony felt proud. He sat against her flank with his head lolled back, taking a grape or two, but mostly waiting.

The grapes gone, Cleo wanted wine. 'But that's locked up,' Anthony said. 'You can't get the key?' she asked. 'I know it's locked up, but you know where the key is. Your mother's so stingy with that wine! You could imagine what happen to me if she ever thought I went into it ... ' Away went Anthony, and while he was seeking the key to wherever the bottle stood, I made one more plea. 'Please, Cleo, can I come some other night?' 'You sure hate to give up,' she laughed. 'Some other night when you're here alone, perhaps ... ?' 'And what will you bring me? Apples? Grapes? I can get all I want of that from your friend. What will you bring?' 'Oranges .. ?' She laughed. 'It's December. That's the only fruit in our yard. Coconuts .. ?' 'Look,' she said, 'I was born right here like you was. You can't bring me something special?' And I knew she wanted me to really promise her Grandfather's money. A new bicycle I had. My fees at the town school were paid, my books bought, and so my clothes, but actual cash — Grandfather was careful to put very little in my hand, and I had no idea where he kept it. I couldn't promise that. Not really. Because then I would have been promising never to come back, and I couldn't promise that. Not ever. 'See?' she said. 'You can't even think of something special to bring me, and you want to come here and stay all night. Want to see what your friend brought last week?' She dipped into her bosom and brought up a little black coin purse from which she took two gold earrings. 'And the week before?' Deeper into the purse to what must have been a piece of high paper money folded into a tight knot. 'And you see for yourself

95

what he's bringing tonight . . . ' 'Doesn't seem all that much . . . ' 'But this way I don't have to steal. He does the stealing, I does the eating, and nobody can't say nothing against me.'

Anthony returned with the wine; a bottle longer, more slender than any I'd ever seen, half full. 'Italian,' he said. Cleo smiled as he passed it to her. She unscrewed the cap and took a gurgling swallow. She took another and another, and in between I had two. Not as long as hers. And Anthony, after worrying for a little as to what they would do with the bottle, he had his third, and the bottle was empty. Cleo lay back, Anthony lolled his head once more. They were both quiet, waiting. And when the silence became overladen with mute wishes, mine the least of the lot, I found that I had pulled myself sufficiently together to leave Cleo and Anthony, leave behind all the rapture I wouldn't have that night.

July 9, Wednesday 10 o'clock

Hille is no Cleo; never could be Cleo. Though in the beginning she was goddess, enchantress, the calypso of my journey which then seemed destined to take me across the seas to those multiple lands where my fragmented self had been scattered. She was the enchantress, I the enchanted, and it had not then occurred to me that whereas I had merely taken the bus from my village to Port-of-Spain, she had made a true journey, complete with ship, ocean, and strange peoples. In reality, then, I was her calypso, but in our early days at the orphanage it seemed otherwise. She was goddess not for me alone, but for the director, staff, and all our black homeless boys as well. The yankee teacher goddess, who brought to our presence, our touch, the living reality of those mythic northerners before whom all nature retreated, against whom paradise had no doors to close. Miss Hille. She belonged to that race out of whose flesh had sprung sky-scrapers, Hollywood, and fighting Joes. Money-littered sidewalks. Non rags, all riches. Her coming had created history. Never before, in all the years of its operation since 1907 had the orphan home been blessed with the presence of an actual goddess, one who not only ate at the same time, the same meals with the staff, but often with a pleasant laugh allowed her pale gold hair to the grimy hands of our boys. As I remember now, we had eyed each other from the beginning, but I was too busy then, along with the others, exhorting the boys to be thankful for having her in their midst — even though it was always impossible to explain to any who asked why — to see what that might lead to. Dreaming, not life, her coming made easier, and how can that be explained to a non-dreamer — that exalted existence in the imagination? Dreaming of her soft white skin myself, and understanding it to be remote, nowhere within my sphere. And so, unlike the others, not scuffling to be in her presence. Wanting, but not daring, since to dare could only be to lose. And losing in the privacy of my room, where the sperm-stiffened sheets were not to be profaned by the touch or vision of others, had become habitual since Cleo. In the beginning I never thought of Hille as having breasts and lips and legs. In my dreams the fusion was always amorphous, a liquid interflow of selves that rose from its own thick beginnings on a colossal flight into the infinite. So that when one day she approached, 'Why do you always eat alone?' it was like seeing for the first time the pin-head freckles beneath the fine hair of her face, and that her teeth were slighly yellow. She was small. Her collar bones punched high beneath the pale skin. I had seen all that before, but it was still seeing like for the first time her water blue eyes that almost matched Grandfather's in depth, except where his were thick viscous pools hers were transparent.

'Why do you always eat alone?' answered by a nervous laugh, a denial. 'I don't always eat alone.' 'I never see you with anyone else. Can I sit down?' 'Please, yes.' In the dingy cafeteria which had perhaps never been repainted since 1907, which certainly had last year's grease clinging to the ceiling and walls, thickest where several generations of flies had been trapped between the bars and metal mesh that covered the windows, I had made it a point to eat always among the last, after the bustle and noise of our hundred boys at midday meal was over. 'You don't live in Port-of-Spain, do you?' 'No. I don't live here.' 'Where do you live?' 'I live in the country, but I only go home on weekends.' 'I bet it's nice there. At least you get away from the awful rooms we have here once in a while.' 'Don't you like your room here?' 'How can anybody like the little closets we have here?' On about staff housing at the orphanage, with which, even though I despised the director who in our eyes was responsible for it, I had never before been dissatisfied. I had not, until Hille mentioned it, realised that my room was too small, too dark a closet, that walls were too thin, the smell from the common lavatory too high. 'In America, God, we would never think of living in a room that didn't have at least one window. I have to leave my door open if I'm to get any fresh air at night. Isn't that a shame? You're lucky to have a place in the country you can go to on weekends.' 'Don't you have any friends away from the orphanage?' 'There are people in town who know my father through his business, but I've only seen them once.' 'No friends at all?' 'Well, the people I know here. The director is very nice, and invites me out often, but I don't feel comfortable with him . . . ' For some strange reason, at that point a great surge of jealousy and rage against the balding, bullet-shaped black man who fulfilled his post with the rigidity and pretentiousness of a rural schoolmaster. Perhaps it is natural that we have latent hostile feelings against our superiors, yet I didn't expect them in her. 'Why don't you feel comfortable with him?' She laughed. 'Maybe if you were a girl you'd understand,' she said. Understand that the little black round-bellied man believed it his ordained privilege to have free access to every female crotch within his environs? It was common knowledge and had never bothered me before, but somehow, at the vision of her in his embrace I was penetrated

98

with a cosmic sense of loss, as though witness and victim of an unleashed and terrible disorder in the universe. The black bull rampant; my calf in danger. There was no reason for me to feel so protective about her. 'And nobody else?' 'I've gone home with some of the girls on weekends, but nobody's ever taken me on a trip outside the city.' The invitation, of course, came to my lips but was not voiced. Instead I talked about my village, tried to describe it so she would know it was not a pretty place. Perhaps I didn't quite make my picture clear. 'Why do you want to leave such a lovely place and come all the way here? Just for the job?' For that, and because Anthony had gone to war, and because of Grandfather, and Cleo, and Betty, but I didn't say any of this. I shrugged instead. Hille said she understood. 'Well, it was nice chatting with you. Don't be such a loner all the time.'

Perhaps we would have lunch at the same hour again soon. We did.

And again.

'I like going to the wharves and watching the ships come in. Do you?' 'I never thought of that as something to do, but it might be fun.' 'You mean your father is a shipowner and you never went down to the sea to watch the ships come in?' 'Well, my father doesn't really own ships, you know. He bought shares in a company that owns them.' 'And that doesn't make him the owner?' 'Not really. When are you going again to the wharves to see them come in?' 'This evening. Would you like to come?' So in time we walked down to the wharves of Port-of-Spain and watched the ships and smelled them, then walked back after the stores were all closed and the only places lit up were the late cafes and the cinemas. All that time we did not touch once, not truly, although we did by accident brush arms once or twice, and I found her skin cold. That very night on the way to Ramjohn's roti shop, and while we waited for him to re-heat the stew prepared especially for tourists, I heard the story of her college days in New England — a long way from Indiana where she was born — where she had an apartment of her own, a motorcar, and all the other luxuries I understood to be commonplace among the daughters of rich Americans. And her boyfriend. I was not prepared for him. I kept a serious mask as she talked about Harry who had graduated a year ahead of her and joined the navy, big strong Harry who always squeezed her tight at football games, Harry the future executive accountant whom she was going to marry when he was through serving the navy, I kept a serious mask. Her Harry sounded very much like Anthony, except bigger and more virile. Where I could conceive of myself as antagonist to Anthony, against Harry such a concept had no beginning. Harry was indeed that great American myth incarnate — the doer of all things, master of men and all phenomena, natural and unnatural — against whose gifts mine of a stroll along the wharves, a snack at Ramjohn's seemed puny. I was so saddened with myself, I paid scant attention then to the words she was saying, and was surprised when she pulled my arm and asked, 'What are you dreaming about? Your girlfriend in the village?' We had left Ramjohn's. I was not dreaming. Re-living instead that moment going on three years in the past when in the presence of Cleo and Anthony I had to hold myself together, keep my shattered pieces in some semblance of an integrated form. 'No. Not dreaming of anyone. I was thinking how nice it is being with you, and we should go out again some time.' I surprised myself. 'Well . . .' she said. 'Is there any reason not to?' 'No, I guess not,' she said. 'All right, then. Tomorrow evening I'll take you to the Gardens.' 'What's that?' 'The Botanical Gardens. Haven't you been there either?' 'No. And after the Gardens where else will you take me?' 'We can go to Carenage, and Maracas, and . . .' 'And your village, some time?' 'Yes.'

The director the next morning calling me to his office to say 'Shepard, you have a good record here with the Home, and I don't want to fire you. But this nonsense you're carrying on with Miss Hille has got to stop. Do you realize what will happen if her father hears of this? He is a rich man. His daughter is teaching here. You know our Home is supported by charity. Put your mind to work, man. What will he think if he hears about her going here and there with you?' I knew. 'Yes, sir.'

The director did not like it, this companionship between rags and riches. So he could go to hell, I thought. But Hille insisted we please him. 'Let's not cause any scandal, okay? If he fires you, everybody will know why.' 'Okay.' So we took to leaving the grounds separately and meeting at pre-designated spots. 'Go for a walk after lights out tonight?' 'Where to?' 'A place I know near Carenage.' 'Tell me how, and I'll meet you there.'

We were not to have a gay time on the dewy hill above Carenage, even with a round yellow moon shining down. We knew. But that did not prevent us from forcing ourselves through the motions. We did not await the moment of true ritual that saves mating from being a gutless empty function. Said Hille when I arrived, 'I was beginning to think you weren't coming.' 'I was giving you time to get here.' 'Giving me time to get here! I left as soon as the lights went out. Where were you?' As usual, when the lights went out I was in my wing of the dormitory, having just finished reading to my boys in bed. The dorm was quiet. Another day's work done, Hille and I alone to come. But it didn't feel right. Maybe it was because of the director, or something about the way Hille insisted he be pleased that kept me standing in the dark dorm disbelieving we would be together in Carenage like other lovers who came there to be alone, be intimate with one another, and only the moon and stars to see. Disbelieving Hille thought of me as lover at all with a vested heart to protect. Yet I had to go, for she would, no doubt. A compact she would never break, and I must do my part. And that was how it was with us without ourselves present forcing it. After a taxi ride through the city to the sea-shore suburb, and then by foot up the dew wet hill, I arrived panting to where she was already waiting to say 'I was beginning to think you weren't coming.' We talked loudly as if there were a great distance between us, even though we were close enough for me to smell lavender or something like it from her hair. The hillside was quiet. The few fishermen's huts between us and the water were dark, and at the base of the hill flashing lights showed where the highway ran back to town. Beyond that and a stretch of mangrove glistening in the moonlight was the broad, light-speckled bay, shifting its vague back constantly. The palms up our slope silently dropped little parasols of moon-shade from which we could choose, but Hille preferred being out in the full light of the moon. 'I've never been in moonlight like this before,' she said. 'In the mid-west we have good moon-light, but nothing as rich and bright as this. I think we can see for miles!' It was true. We could see the lights of Carrera, and past the other tiny islands all the way to the distant, hulking mainland. 'Have you ever been to Venezuela?' she asked. 'No.' 'Wouldn't you like to?' 'I'd like to go someday.' 'You ought to just take up and go.' 'How do you mean "just take up and go"?' 'Well, just go down to the boat office, buy yourself a ticket and hop aboard. Don't they have boats that sail from here to Venezuela?' 'Yes, they have boats, but I can't just walk down there and get on one.' 'Not before you get a ticket.' 'I can't just do that.' 'What? Get a ticket?' 'Yes.' 'Why not?' 'Well, I can't. Not just like that.' 'You're a free man, aren't you? If you want to take a boat ride who is to stop you?' 'Nobody. But I can't.' 'You mean you don't really want to; isn't that it?' And for that I had no answer, having long dreamed of seeing the mainland, seeing it come close, close enough to lose me in its jungles, feather me into cities where Latin music seeped from every crevice, where the sun climbed and fell each day to an erotic throb, but never having thought of going down to the boat office and buying a ticket just like that. Somehow that seemed too simple, too unremarkable a beginning to the great breaking away I dreamed would one day mark the business of my real life.

'Besides, I would have to get a passport and visas, and all that. It's a lot of trouble.' 'I had to get a passport and visa and all kinds of vaccinations too. It wasn't that much trouble.' 'You don't know how hard it is to get anything done here. This isn't America.' 'Maybe I could help you if you really wanted to go.' I was not making myself clear. Best then to be silent. 'Let's sit down,' she said. 'The ground's wet.' 'It doesn't matter.' For of course she had her cloak, a fine tan gaberdine that shone almost as much as her hair as she spread it over the dew grass. We sat. The moon was a powerful green, reflected off the palm fronds, ground, and anything else touched. Even the shadows were like turgid algae pools shifting slightly with the swaying of the trees. Hille's dress was a smooth pale green. Her bare legs and arms, her face, also green. Up to beneath the skin, green without glowing. The moonlight said Hille's hands were green, definitely green, as were mine, only mine were a few shades greener so they were very near to black. And above the palm tops the night was somewhat golden, and higher yet the sky was like blue milk and everything was shiny. 'Moonlight makes everything so soft,' she said. 'Makes me so soft inside. Doesn't it you?' she asked, inclining her lavender scented head towards my shoulder but not touching. 'Sometimes.' 'This is the sort of night makes a girl want to be careful. Are you angry about something?' 'No.' 'Oh. You're so quiet.' 'I'm thinking.' 'Oh!' Trying to think, really. The lavender head was too close. The scent kept sucking my stomach up towards open air, sucking streaks of bile into my mouth before I could swallow back. Trying to think into the right moment for putting an arm around her; but that moment never came. I did put my arm around her, and felt her stiffen. Nothing else. I later took one of her green hands into my greener hand, and it came as only a little ball of warm meat from which all the nerves had been drawn back. And later still, after she drew the green dress up over her green legs, giving up a fresh cloud of lavender, and lay carefully back on the khaki-tan cloak, the warm ball of meat changed places, and that was all. Except, finally, a massive rush of bile, more than my mouth could hold, forced up through my nose and I had to heave. Had to leave off fingering Hille for a minute or two of retching. Which she withstood without comment, with only the pulling down of her dress and sitting up with her head tossed back as if waiting for an apology. I didn't know what to say.

Then Hille wanted to remain alone on the hillside for a while, but I said no. It was late and that would be too dangerous. She insisted. She wanted to be left alone in the quiet. 'How do you think it makes me feel to have you get sick like that?' 'I'm all right now. I'm sorry it happened. Let's go down and get a taxi back to town.' 'Tell me. I want to know. What happened? Was it something I did?' 'No, nothing you did. It won't happen again.' 'You mean we won't come here again?' 'No, I don't mean that.' 'It is such a lovely night; I'm sorry you got sick. Next time tell me what it is I shouldn't do.' 'Wasn't anything you did . . .' '. . . or if it was something I said . . .' 'No, no. It's all right. Won't happen again. Let's go down.' What else could I say, with my mind short-circuited, my stomach still roily from the smell of lavender?

We came down the hillside hand in hand, our flanks occasionally pressed together; and back at the orphanage I said she should go before, but she refused. We walked through the gates still hand in hand, and in the centre of the scruffy courtyard she stopped to look up at the moon and say, 'It was still a lovely night. Next time don't forget to tell me what I must say and do. Okay?' 'Okay. Next time.' She to her room, and I to mine hoping the round-bellied director had been somewhere snooping so he could overhear the last words.

Continued then, our habit of leaving the grounds separately; but after a while we met at a single pre-designated place — my room on George Street, our room on George Street, paid for by the shining American enchantress whom my body understood was not quite that, but whom my mind kept insisting

104

had to be. Paid for by her to that crafty cynic, The Undertaker, That amputated vulture who sits still in his window exactly the way he sat when we came along to look at the room that day. 'Sweethearts?' was his first question. 'No,' Hille said swiftly. 'Just friends. We need a good room for Marcus. With two windows, if you have one.' 'Would one window do?' It would. And then his offering us the key in his outstretched hand which was quite brown and gnarled, and looked as though it had squeezed the life out of many a throat in its day. But that came after our day at the seashore, which was a more successful venture than the night, and in some ways an echo of that fatal meeting between Anthony, Hille, and myself, although it took place sooner.

'Ever since I was a little girl I've wanted to see the tropics. See what real black people were like. There was a black family in the town where I grew up but they weren't the real thing. They were just regular niggers. Nice though. The man was a preacher; used to be gone from his family all weekend to preach at the nigger church up in the city slums. He had a nice daughter though. She went to our high school and you could hardly tell she was there. We never had any trouble with her. But they weren't real black people — like Africans or you. Weren't really niggers either, come to think of it. I used to dream of going to Africa, and when my father stopped selling insurance and bought into the steamship company I wanted to go right away, but he said I had to finish college first. Then he said I should get some experience in my field while I was still young so I started teaching right after college. Then he said he didn't think I should go quite so far as Africa all alone — although I really think he didn't want to put out the money — why didn't I try the West Indies. I hadn't even thought of that. I never even thought that right here in our own tropics we had real black men and women who were so different from the niggers at home. So it didn't matter if my father was really being stingy, he scored a winner there. I'm glad I came. Are you?'

It was our second venture, our daytime at the sea, and the sucking vacuoles, I had them clamped against nausea. The sea lapped outside beneath our window, and wherever the room's dingy boards had curled away from each other little streaks of noon-time sun came darting through — pencil probes into the dim interior. 'Well, are you?' 'I am very glad you came.' And she wanted me to say more, but I didn't; listened instead for another time to how she had always wanted to work with poor black children, and when her boat docked at Port-of-Spain the first thing she did was ask where was the vocational school, only here it's not called that, it's called an orphan home instead. How she adored the little black darlings with their flashing smiles and dirty hands . . . 'But not as much as I adore you, dear. Were you like that when you were growing up?' 'I suppose so.' 'Did you dance and play all the time the way they do? I bet you were always into something.' 'Like what?' 'For you, I bet it was girls. I bet you started with girls early.' At that I had to laugh. 'Did you ever bring any of your old sweethearts to this hotel?' Me who had never been to a hotel before, would never have thought of going to one nor even then gone had she not suggested, effected an arrangement which asked only that I be at the given address before noon on our Saturday off. The first Saturday off I was not on my way to the village. In time to become a habit. 'Did you ever?' 'No. Never before.' 'This is the first time?' 'The first time.' 'You're hot.' I was hot, and concentrating on keeping my bile in its place. Every damned thing was hot. The bare little bureau with discoloured pages of an ancient *Evening News* lining its drawers; that, and the creaky old bedstead hardly big enough for two had long ago been heated to discolouration; and the heat was sweating us now, making us sticky-damp where we touched, making us add many drops to those already stained into the splotch-patched sheet. While the sea washed steadily below, sending up the smell of tar. Black tar and funk and stale saltiness, swirling odours in the room. But there was no nausea. In fact, feeling ourselves both present I found my body moved by Hille, and a little joy crept in between us this second time. I thought of Harry once, and, strange, her being naked beneath me did not seem much of a victory over him. The effect was to diminish his presence altogether, but bring home sharply how far she and I must go if . . . if — I will not let myself say what comes behind that if. I am now ashamed of it.

Our joy did not last when we took it into the open air of the verandah. Out there, a flat-edged galvanized awning gave narrow protection from the afternoon sun, but there was nothing to shield us from the slant glare coming off the water, off the white-walled next door hotel, off the sails puttering about in the Gulf, the gulls and hulls of parked boats, off every conceivable object within vision. We were sitting then in swimsuits with two frosty bottles of beer between us, and Hille's face, the whole front of her was red from the heat and embracing. Her eyes shined a little, and her hair blew away soft and wavy. Her lips made a line that said they were pleased, satisfied. I had put it there — the little sparkle in the eye, the repose of the lips and brow. We were alone on the verandah. I touched her hand. We knew what together meant, our fingers said. Until four brawny sailors trooped their way up on to the verandah from the bar, and we were no longer alone. Yankees from the nearby naval base; and one said, looking square at Hille and me, 'Is that one of our niggers?' 'Sit down, Tom. Leave him alone.' 'He looks like one of our niggers. So help me if he is . . .' 'Sit down, Tom. He ain't none of our boys. You know they know better than to be seen with no nigger-loving bitches. Sit down.' 'Who is that bitch?' 'Sit down . . .' 'Back in Carolina, do you know what we would do to you?' (To Hille.) 'Don't know 'bout Carolina, but tell you what we'd do in Illinois — take her out and feed her to the boars!' They laughed. Harry's navy. While I pretended to hearing not a word, pretended that the laughing sun-red faces three yards away were as oblivious of me as I wished to be of them. But our fingers fell apart, Hille's and mine. I sipped my beer, and Hille hers, and she was pretending not to have heard a word about nigger-loving bitches either, I could tell, though she did sit a little straighter, and the red down her face spread around her neck and up into her hair. Then suddenly she said out loud, 'How come black men are so much better than white men?' I pretended not to hear her either. 'How come black men are so free?' she continued. One of them said, 'D'you hear that bitch?' They stopped chatting and laughing and were silent. 'How come black men have such beautiful free bodies?' she asked, her voice tinkling clearly on each word. 'What are you asking me about black men for?' I muttered. 'You have the most beautiful body,' she said, reaching for my hand, and I feel a little redeemed by what my face in that moment must have said, for suddenly she blanched and said, 'Don't you look at me like that! Don't you dare look at me like that! Talk to me.'

Thursday July 10, 1952

In 1943 there was a war. Our village had known in a slight way before that there was, but in 1943 we knew for real, because it made us fight like beasts among ourselves whenever the Chinese shop got in a sack or two of rice or lentils, a barrel of pickled meat. In the dark hours before dawn we formed lines outside the town bakery that stretched past the police station and hospital, to wait for bread. We stood in line and hoped that the sun did not catch us still waiting, for that would mean another breadless day. And not only did we know there was a war because of the shortage of rice and peas and bread, the noisy fighting over each catch brought in by the fishermen; at night, whether there was a moon or not, Anthony's father rolled up and down the village road in his jitney — palm bedecked so as to make it camouflaged — wearing the helmet which said 'Air Raid Warden' on the front, shouting wherever he saw a flicker, 'Dim that light.' Once in a while we would even hear the drone of a single plane coming towards the factory, and leave our darkened rooms to cluster outside and watch the surrounding searchlights sweep the sky to find it. Air-raid practice. Eventually, a recruiting officer came to sign up volunteers, and, in the name of George VI, installed himself in the lodge building of The Hand of Justice Friendly Benevolent Society with a folding table and matching chair, and a sign tacked up inviting all those who were loyal to the honour of the King and the glory of the British Empire to come forward and register their lives against the heinous Axis barbarians who wished to catapult the whole world into slavery.

'Slavery!' Grandfather laughed. As did some others among the Saturday morning old-timers sipping the first one in the shade of the rumshop. 'They have the gall to be talking about fighting against slavery — after what they did to Marcus Garvey!' 'Ain't that the truth?' 'When is somebody going to come free the slaves they got in this village?' 'Yes, when? That I'd like to know.' 'They the biggest slave holders in the world.' 'That's true.' 'Well, hold on now, Pappa Jay, you forgetting Queen Victoria and Wilberforce? You forgetting your history?' 'That's right. We got to pay attention to the history. In 1863 Queen Victoria freed all the slaves.' 'Freed the slaves? You're crazy. They got slaves right here in this village, they got them all over the West Indies, and Africa, and India, and you come telling me some queen or the other freed the slaves?' 'Man, we're free. We ain't nobody's slaves.' 'Just the same, Pappa Jay right. Ain't nobody calling us slaves, but what is we? You look at them redfaces living across the pond then look at us. What are we?' 'Well you ain't no white man, that's for sure.' 'You damn right we ain't no white mens, and as long as you're black you're a slave.' 'Tha's going too far. What I mean is, remember how you used to run like hell to catch that seven o'clock whistle every morning?' 'Yes, so what? A man's got to work.' 'All right. But isn't there something wrong with a man tucking his tail in and behaving like he's going get a whipping because he's just a minute behind the whistle?' 'Well, what d'you expect? If you're late you're late. You're working for somebody.' 'That's just what I mean. You're working for somebody, not yourself. Twelve hours in the factory, sometimes more than that in the field. And any time the white man's got his eyes on you you tuck your head down low and hope he doesn't send you home. Now ain't that slavery?' 'That ain't no slavery, that's work. That's how you make your living.' 'I know it's work. They know it too. That's why they don't do much of it. Yet they eat Sunday dinners every day, and throw away more clothes than you can buy in a lifetime. They don't have to starve to buy a bicycle, their son ride to school in a car. In England they have it better still off the sweat we put down. That ain't slavery?' 'I don't know about you, but I's a free man. Nobody tell you to work for the white man if you don't want to.' 'That's right. Nobody told me to work for the white man. But tell me something, you know a one of us who wasn't born scared? As long as you're scared you're a slave.' 'You talking about being scared. If you find life so hard with the white man why didn't you join up with Marcus Garvey?' 'I did. I was ready to go back to Africa, still ready. But Marcus Garvey wasn't going nowhere. I knew the white man wasn't going to let him get back there. You want to know why?' 'You talking.' 'That would have meant war. If ever they let us take back what we know to Africa, it would mean war. And not no pissing tail checker board war either — real war! Now then, don't that make you scared?' 'Scared of what? Chuts man, if I had to fight I'd fight.' 'Yeah, you're saying that now. But we've done imagined what it will be like; that's why we're never going get up and fight. Can you imagine? All of Africa rising up, and here, and in North America, Brazil, everywhere, black men rising up behind one national anthem. That would be a formidable sight to see! But a whole lot would get killed too. A whole lot.' 'That's right.' 'I stopped dreaming about that kind of rising up ever since they got Marcus Garvey. But that don't mean I'm going fight on their side in any other war either. Chuts, the Germans no worse than the English. They're all white.' 'That's what I'm saying. This ain't no war for black people. And if I had a son was going up there to sign his name volunteering, I'd kill him myself.' Listening to Grandfather's voice thinking, old man, you're just an old man. Wouldn't it be grand to join the army and fight against the German barbarians? It would be grand to be in battle against them, or any other enemy, especially in a crisp uniform, giving orders, leading my men in charge after charge against their guns and bayonets; perhaps, certainly, winning the DSM. For when in school we sang 'Britons never never shall be slaves' I was a Briton, and it never occurred to me that Britain had yet to acknowledge the existence of black Britons. I was one, with bayoneted rifle slung across my shoulder, tramping forth to the glory of King and Empire. My comrades were of course all Tommies, with their chin straps snug, and written across their faces — victory or death. Only death never figured in. And whatever glory I won, though first to the honour of King and Empire, in extension for myself too. A hero. Standing without a word in the drench of rum fumes, listening to Grandfather, an old man's voice jarring against my battle winning dreams. The town newspapers carried every day accounts of sixteen-year-old English boys flying planes. Trapped in the midst of these lean-shanked, curl-toed men who would never handle guns, who would never fly planes, who would never ever know what it was to march in an army — except on anniversary Sundays when The Hand of Justice Friendly Benevolent Society behind a hired marching band minced in shoes too infrequently worn, sweltered in the black 'occasion' suits that buttoned either too easily or too tightly. That was their army — 'Onward Christian soldiers, marching as to war ...' — the women singing louder than the men. A metaphor. They could deal with that. Not the real thing. How to do anything but despise the old men for their narrow minds, their fear, and rum-soaked pugnacity? They stood like a black wall between me and

III

glory, while perhaps in that very moment Anthony was being sent off with his father's blessings.

Grandfather had no blessings to give in this regard, not even on the night when Anthony had his public send-off. Amidst the turn-out in the lodge building on a rainy night, practically the whole village there — except the gamblers, and Grandfather, and a few of his old friends — to give a public 'God bless you' to Anthony and two other village sons, all three sitting stiffly in new uniforms upon the stage; and to hear old redface tell us how the British Empire was a glorious achievement, and how we should all be prepared to die to defend it. Sugar was a vital product. A great producer of energy; a basic food for all living beings. Without it, all civilization would definitely wither up and pass away. We had a commitment to win the war against the barbarians; and although we could not take part in the actual fighting, we were to support our fighters by producing more sugar — putting in longer hours in the fields, and making every minute of every day count in the factory. As to our own fighting men, the three before us, they took with them the honour of our village. A serious charge, which they would find not easy, but which they may under no circumstances cast off. To his boy, a further privilege — that of protecting the tradition of his ancestors, of offering his most personal and unique possession, life, to protect those traditions from all barbarisms now and in the future. Feeling bad. Looking at the three of them on stage, and feeling bad, both for myself and the two others. For whereas Anthony shone, his uniform with its brass buttons giving colour to his red face, his finely shaped head seemingly satisfied to be on its shoulders, the other two were dull. Their heads had little outline against the backdrop, and the running black of their dense faces trickled down, infected even the stiff uniforms they wore, so that the cloth and buttons lost all sparkle and the suits seemed little more than uncomfortable dark rags about their shoulders. Wouldn't I have cut a far more respectable figure? Wouldn't I have been a respectable match for Anthony? It meant nothing that my face was as black as theirs, or that my head too would have been lost against the backdrop. I would have been his equivalent in the training camp to which they were headed, or in an enemy city where the fighting was swift, hard, made to order only for conquerors.

'You are not a white man,' Grandfather bellowed later that night when he found me crying. 'You don't have any damn sense. Let the English and the Germans kill off one another — you're no damned white man.' Scolding not enough to stop the crying. White or not I could be a hero. And if he were not in the way, he and all the other grandfathers who sweated out their lives in fear, with a trust in vengeance, if they with their vengeful glances at the white man's back but tucked in heads when he approached were not in the way, the whole hot black village not in the way, I could reach up and be more than just a man — a hero. 'That man's blood is your blood,' he shouted, pointing again to the book with his old slave. 'It runs in your veins, and all your educating and church-going can't change that.' The book in his hands now. How often had we come to that? This frayed, blackened, greasy book, lugged from Barbados, to Curaçao, to Maracaibo, to wherever else he had landed before coming down for good in Trinidad; this book which over and over again he asserted held the key to my ancestry? The photographs in it, none looked like me. Especially of the one he called his father. It looked the most alien of all. 'Look at his brow, it has the breadth of nobility. His eyes shine with the wisdom of kings . . .' and all I could see was a withered old man whose head was remarkable only for its bluntness. A black broad skull, and flying nostrils, eyes not only docile but pleading, a neck and limbs shrivelled, as though the body's vitality had already leaked out into somewhere outside the picture. If there were anything noble about my great-grandfather then this certainly couldn't be he. This old slave was whipped. 'Adolphus soon after coming to the house of Shepard', that's

113

what his caption said. And further on in the book was another photograph of Adolphus, this time with grey hair, a white tunic, and an apologetic smile on his face — a whipped man who knew he had been whipped, apologizing for something or other that did not show in the photograph. Not my great-grandfather. 'That's your great-grandfather, boy. That's your blood. And all your educating can't make no white man out of you. Stop your crying! You ain't going to no war. Get your tail in there and learn how to read and count and write! That's your war.' So Anthony went to war, but I stayed home to learn how to read and write and count; and eventually make that shipless trip from my village to the orphan home an adventurous fifty miles away.

In the year when Anthony should have been finishing school he was away fighting in the war; or, at any rate, away doing something because of the war. And Cleo was gone, had been gone, from his father's house to another redface who was a young bachelor, she let everybody know, from somewhere in Wales. She was his only servant — maid, cook, and woman. No one disbelieved her. The village men whom her Eccles over-seered all agreed he became a softer man to work under after Cleo went to his house, and it was even conjectured that Anthony's father purposefully gave her up to the new man, because the redfaces on the other side of the pond were — from the very first day Eccles showed up flexing his broad hairy calves beneath khaki shorts that were shorter, tighter than any worn by the other overseers, a smile to beat the devil across his face pink not only in the cheeks, but glowing all across the forehead as well except where a thin white line separated it from his wavy auburn hair — anxious, because he wore so many signs of the unpredictable, the intractable. So they gave him Cleo, the way a wild boar is fed a sow or two to tame him, and after a while the other redfaces didn't have to keep such a sharp eye on Eccles any more, nor the men who worked under him either, and no one disbelieved Cleo when at those extraordinary times when a pig or goat was slaughtered and everyone clamoured around for a piece of meat she shouted, 'No bones, no fat! I want the best. My man don't eat nothing but the best!' And if the other women shoved her out of place, then all she did was tiptoe and wave her redface's dollar bills above the heads of them all, and got what she wanted.

It was enough to make a body cry who had sat with Cleo in the dark and felt her hand and her hot breath coming like a volcano in which you could be devoured forever. It was enough to make a body cry the way she became so remote, so untouchable, consumed solely in this red-legged man with his perpetual grin that bared two rows of savage teeth but never touched his eyes. So that even before Anthony went away because of the war he seemed given to a continuous crying that kept his eyes sombre and vacantly focused. At school he walked hunched over as though trying to compensate for that same hollowness I felt in the middle but would not show. He gave up his bicycle, and with his brother who had lately started at the high school sat emptily in the Company car that took them back and forth, morning and afternoon. It would have been nice to give up my bicycle too, but I had no car; and each afternoon then I was left behind, and any racing was completely out of the question. It was in those days that I was found by Stone who picked me up and decided to make me his brother.

Just as well. No car, and Cole forked by two broad red legs. Stone the gambler! Two or three years older, recently grown out of the ragged pants that left half his bottom bare, 'All you have to do is be a winner.' he said. 'Is that all?' 'Sure! Here, let me show you how to make the dice work.' And he made them work. Sevens and elevens, sixes, eights, snake eyes, whatever he wanted — he made them work. 'See? It's easy,' he said. But it wasn't easy when I tried, and nothing worked. 'You have to practise,' he said. 'It's the same with cards. You just have to practise.' He had to be right too, because he had become the peer of all the village gamblers ancient and new; he could match them at whatever game they chose, and beat them often enough to drop his rags for well-tailored gaberdines and satin shirts. 'All you have to do is practise. Come on, I'll show you how.' Without any explanation of why he had chosen me. We had never idled together, because I had never idled; we had never gone to school together, because he had never gone to school. Yet, 'Come on, I'll show you how,' a face I knew as village faces can't help knowing each other, one of those with a voice behind it waiting at the centre of the village when Anthony and I raced through.

Stone. Gambler, village lover — every winner had to be — and would-be big brother. Against Grandfather's wishes. Grandfather who believed a daily nip had the virtue of preserving the brain, and that pleasing women was a duty placed upon all men by the Almighty from puberty to the last purging erection, but who harangued that there could be none but the most abominable values to gambling, inasmuch as the only pleasure it gave rested upon another man's losses. And, fundamentally, I must have believed him, although on occasion I dreamed that magical feeling of myself going down, pleasurably losing, going down, the touching sweetness of seeing the thing most wanted enjoyed by another while longing for the day when it would come and remain in my hands forever. The sweet tragicness of dreams frustrated beforehand. But that would have to come from the other side, not Stone's side, because he was not a loser. And fundamentally I must have agreed with Grandfather, because I never learned how to make either dice or cards work. Nor people either — though I tried. So that one dark Lenten night that year, when the thick stars pulsed to the crickets' chirping, and one recognized others passed along the road by listening to the characteristics of their feet — Margie with the clubfoot, Mongo with the dragging heels, Tits with each foot falling forcefully and independent — with the whole village singly, in twos or threes on its way to church, even the children, playing hide and seek along the dark road between their parents' legs, everybody on the way to church for Wednesday night was magic lantern night, and there would be many strange pretty pictures from the Bible flashing on the screen temporarily hung just below the chancel, everybody on their way to church, except Grandfather who tolerated my going only because I had been at it so long before coming to live with him, and the gamblers, who instead were gathered in the parlour shooting billiards. There was no darkness in their hangout. Its Coleman lantern gave off light enough to brighten every corner, then send yellow shafts slanting through the open doors as well, the only light that crossed the village road, except for an occasional bus or Company car so that walkers on their way to church or elsewhere once they came around the bend to the billiard parlour walked lighter with their eyes fast on the light, and when they came to it slowed down, straining their necks to see who gambled in the brilliance of that magnificent Coleman, slowed down to let the light relieve for a moment the tension of their eyes, let it brighten up the corners of their dark dusty faces, before passing on into the darkness again. I stopped. Foremost among the gamblers that night was Stone, his flowered satin shirt sweat-streaked down the middle of the back, crouched over the table preparing to make a stroke. Stone, the neo-success of the village, the one currently to make village women cry. He was my friend. How many times had he said, 'Boy, you'll never be a gambler. You have the right kind of fingers, but you'll never be a gambler. You're more cut out to be a doctor. Tell me all that stuff about the leaf again. You know how many grown women never heard about leaves breathing and things like that?' So repeat what the textbook said about stomata, and CO_2, and chlorophyll, until Stone thought it time to make a parallel. 'That's just like a woman! Did you know women breathe through their breasts? A lot of men don't know that. But I'm telling you. One of these days when you get it right you'll see for yourself — those breasts breathing and sucking on your chest, man, nothing like it!' Then to be told about women. But telling nothing about Cleo.

Stone made his stroke, then two or three more, and the other gamblers shaking their heads let him have their money. From further down the road the church bell had rung and stopped for the third time, and the road was empty now, save for a few who hurried not to miss any of the magic lantern. 'You ready to get it tonight?' Stone coming up, smiling, in a gay mood, still putting away the money he had just won, rank with sweat and coconut-oil and Yardley's cologne. 'You ready to get it tonight little bo?' Hell bent-on keeping his big-brotherly pro-mise to instruct me in the handling of real womanhood. 'She's waiting now right where I told her.' She being any young unhusbanded or even husbanded female of the village, any female of the village, almost, that Stone had promised to see that night. 'She'll be waiting.' Assured, brotherly. With an assurance never known when it was going to see Cleo. With a dryness, where going to see Cleo would have been fearful, and hopeful, and sweet, but sad, and real and dreaming all at the same time. A dryness. Assured. 'That chemistry and biology in school is all right — you're going to be a doctor. But you can't forget the real thing. You're running too far behind right now. You ready?' As though I were a racehorse, and he the trainer-groom, and here at last the perfect moment in which to break myself in on a real track. And was I ready? Ready for what? Something I kept trying to think must be like Cleo, only I knew it couldn't be because it felt and sounded dry. 'She'll be waiting right where I told her.' And into the night we sortied, past the church, set back between its tall palms almost into the edge of the canefield that was newly cut, where the congregation was singing the second hymn. And I should have been there to swing the incense before each station. That didn't bother me much. In my heart a sad spot for each magic lantern picture I would not see — that bothered. But on, past the church, across the bridge spanning the stinking factory river, past the covered grandstand above the cricket ground — but not quite past that. Deftly in the dark Stone left the road. We climbed a pile of sand bricks, me following purely by feel, and then we descended on the other side, Stone finding a slide board that let us into the pavilion, and there she was; rising up darker in the darkness, saying 'Stone?' A voice I did not dare for a moment believe. 'Stone, you come?' None other. Betty. The same from earlier days when the Reverend-tutor moaned like a stuck pig out of breath, who since the generous traveller had gone away was in Anthony's father's house, where she had taken her sister's place. 'Who's that with you?' 'Marcus.' 'Marcus? Oh him. What did you bring him for?' 'He's my little brother. Wherever I go, he goes.' 'I can't stay long.' 'Well what you doing standing up talking?' Into a silence during which I couldn't quite see what they were doing. Until footsteps stirred and started down the wooden steps, Stone calling, 'Come on little brother.' Following, not wanting to get too close; and when they came to a place where the folding chairs were broken, the platform boards bare and smooth, they stopped. Stopping too, but not too close; close enough to hear the murmur of their voices but not understand their words. To hear the rustle of clothes in the dark, and, 'Come on little brother. You scared?' 'Scared of what?' And Betty, 'It's not as if I could stay out all night.' Not scared, just the feel of that total dryness in my mouth and throat, my nostrils too until she laughed and came a hand descending on me. Going forward on my knees not fully crying, not fully conscious of the drag along hard boards, not fully anything, except a hand, not Cleo's hand on my crotch, and I couldn't allow that. To feel my body flinch and recoil, and hear myself groping away, and finally Stone saying, 'A man's always scared the first time, but don't let that stop you.' And Betty's tinkling laugh, as though it no longer mattered that she couldn't stay out late; laughing and coaxing, 'What you afraid of me for? You know me . . .' Not scared. Just not wanting to be there, and sad at all the magic lantern pictures being missed. 'You shut up,' said Stone. 'Leave him alone and take care of me.' Withdrawing on my knees to my former place, looking away in the dark, hearing but not hearing the platform boards squeak behind my ear, hearing but not clearly Stone and Betty doing whatever they had to do. Apart from them, clearly, a voice that would be mine if I let it, 'I could have had Betty if I really wanted her. Didn't want her.' My voice, but going away, going down beneath Betty's, feeling and losing with her, perhaps crying too. A performance Grandfather no doubt never would have understood; but for a few years afterwards I could say in my own voice, 'I could have had Betty if I had really wanted her.' Recovering eventually, enough to carry myself back on my feet through the dark night to the cluster of noiseless palms between which the church sat like an overgrown yet humble chicken coop. Wriggling my way to a window, I who should have been part and parcel of the spectacle within, wriggling in between the vagrants, idlers, others who habitually had no use for church, who on Sundays and feast days preferred lolling in the almond shade next to the cricket ground, or in the shade of the rumshop eaves with dice and drum. Standing between them half lost in the tall dew grass beneath the window, nose fixed to the dusty diamond-shaped panes, eyes beyond that to the white makeshift screen dangling before the chancel with its magic coloured pictures coming, standing, going. Not being able to stop my eyes from roving into the empty pews in the dim alcove of the chancel itself, for there is where I should have been sitting earlier, among the choir boys in our cassocks and white surplices; not being able either to help seeing the first pews beneath the pulpit where, even in the vague configurations of the dimly lit congregation, a filled out row of redfaces showed clearly, erect, with no intrusion between them and the long canvas screen before the chancel gate. Certainly Anthony must have been among them. There was his place. Not only was his place among them in the front row of the church, but suddenly it was there too in the centre of the screen as well, a little older, terribly strained, and horror struck, but definitely himself, Anthony, at the centre of the oblong tableau, trapped by his hair, flowing golden hair flowing up into the tangled oak tree dragging the rest of his dangling self after it, that self which rebelled from the hair roots downwards in furious agony and helplessness. It sent a quiver through me to see him hanging there, especially as he was not alone, instead had for company the grim bearded assailant who had just delivered the final of three thrusting darts that protruded like indifferent handholds in case one wished to climb up the body. Anthony skewered in a tangled oak. 'Absalom, Absalom, my son!' the caption. Far sharper than the sword thrust of Good Friday. Preparation the difference. Preparation for a calm face, a face beyond agony, sculptured and serene, with no screaming eyes. No terror. Preparation for the grave moment beyond agony; no screaming eyes, no matter what skewers, or bludgeons or whatever came at the arm of justice. Anthony trapped in a moment without preparation, suffering the three darts, helpless to defend himself. I quivered, then cried. I should never grow a beard to fall upon my chest, nor grow hair long enough to wrap around the boughs of an oak. Yet knowing I was the same as one or the other, bearded or long-haired; knowing Anthony, adoze as he was in the first pew beneath the pulpit was one or the other too. Cried from feeling doomed, sensing the uselessness of, 'Lord have mercy upon us, Christ have mercy upon us', sensing mercy to be more remote than that, remote, perhaps never to come out of the most obscure corners of the universe. Taking up a heavy walk home in the dark night; coming, long after Anthony with the others of his family had raised a funnel of dust down the road in their private Company car, coming to the billiard parlour with its slash of green light striking out into the darkness, where among the gamblers, all gabbling from their glistening faces, stood Stone in a fresh shirt now, propped in the doorway with a toothpick to his lips like a man who had just devoured the most delicious morsel in town. 'Marc! Hey Marc!' Calling. 'Little brother . . .' But I pretended not to hear and hurried on through the light. Coming, jogging from behind, 'So you went to church then?' 'Mmm Hmm.' 'Say, you want a dollar?' 'Mmm Hmm.' 'Go on. Take it. Buy something. And say, you know if you ever want to see her by yourself all you have to do is let me know. Any time. You understand? Don't worry about what happened tonight. Next time I'll let you take her up to the grandstand alone, and you'll be ready. Okay?' 'I don't want to see . . .' 'Don't worry, you will. And once you get a taste of that sweetness, man . . . ! Okay? Any time you're ready. And don't feel bad when you see her on the street. I warned her not to have anything to say to you. Okay . . . ?'

How to explain to Stone that it was not the thought of passing Betty on the street — even though that was bad enough — nor the memory of myself crawling away on hands and knees along the dark pavilion floor? How to explain the presence of death in the air, death at the hands of bearded men, and on the faces too of all the others standing around the window with the dew grass up to their hips, and on the gamblers' faces despite their loud talk and late village laughter, and on Stone's face too, toothpick, heavy black eyes and all. Stop! Tell them all to stop! But in a useless voice, because on the next morning when the whole village roused by the cries of the milkman rushed to the pasture adjacent to the dairy, and there gathered around the single mango tree which stood like a stunted umbrella in the open field, Stone was the first to keep saying, 'Man, that'll never happen to me. Nothing in this world could make me kill myself.' And unknown why the Indian boy killed himself. Unknown why he was swinging there with the rope gouged deep behind his ear, probably having said to many of the others gathered there beneath his swaying corpse just that, 'Nothing in the world could make me kill myself.' Everyone speculating, discovering, that although Boodram was a village son nobody knew him past the surface, nobody knew what rage, what despairing details emptied him of the wish to live, and even so, many still not caring, convinced explanation was a racial trait — 'coolies are forever hanging themselves' — and that was all. Running over the same ground one had covered to see Thunder, running now to see a dead man one barely knew — a face among village faces, where the same faces occur every day — a man who despite the sameness of his everydays had kept a terrible secret locked up inside him that he had left us now to decipher. 'Man, nothing in the world could make me kill myself.' With the sun just coming over the morning cloud bank, a dead man twirling now east, then west. A cipher. Two dead eyes bulging, like a grotesque clown. A grotesque clown. Random voices ask, as if I should know, 'Why do you suppose he did it?' 'How do you suppose he climbed so high in the dark?' Christ, if you watched a tree long enough you could climb it in the dark without eyes, without mind, if you really wanted to. And, 'Do you think it took him long to die?' If you're so curious, why don't you try it yourself? 'When a man is hung his tongue usually falls out. How come his doesn't?' Christ almighty, I've never hung myself yet. So his tongue stayed in, but something else came out, and it stained his pants both in front and behind for everyone to see. 'I'll never hang myself. Never,' Stone saying, and random voices pick it up, 'Me neither . . .' '. . . a gun, or a dagger, or throw myself in the pond . . .' But never hang ourselves, never, as it came time to leave the pasture, time for school.

On an afternoon in 1945 we had a band half the village long raising such a racket with its makeshift instruments that if the Germans had not already surrendered, the celebration we raised might have brought a bomb faster than all the lamps we had not lit over the past four years. Even Grandfather came out and danced down the road, although he had to keep saying, 'If it weren't for them Yanks, we'd be celebrating the Germans right now.' The factory gave its workers a day off and Anthony's father handed out victory flags. Outside the school the children lined up to sing 'Rule Britannia' and 'Siegfried Line' and 'You're a Sap Mr Jap', before scampering into the road with their bottle and spoons to join the dancing. The church bell rang long and loud, and Mr Stephen, the sexton, afterwards said that the ringing worked up several blisters on his hand but that that was all right, because he was very happy the war was over and no fighting would ever come to Trinidad. And long after darkness that day, the Chinese rumshop was still open, the police station closed, while the jangling band danced from one end of the village to the other.

We were all happy that the war had been won — even the old men who had hoped the Germans and English would kill each other off — because it meant less fighting among ourselves over a sack of flour, a barrel of saltfish, and, especially for those young like me, it meant the discovery of a new band of heroes — the Yanks. These mythical warrior men, brave, daring, and generous as well, had helped, had won the war for Britain. Everywhere Yanks were the rage. What're you going to be when you grow up boy? Robert Taylor in *Bataan*. I'm going to be John Wayne in *Flying Tigers*. I'm going to be Humphrey Bogart in *Sahara*! We were all very happy, proud too that these modern legendaries were up out of our very own ocean, a stone's throw across the water as these things go, and in some way, through the agency of neighbourhood perhaps, felt ourselves related to, a part of, this New World myth. And in myself, the discovery of another land to which I was spirit bound, so that the envisioned journey to collect all fragments of the self into a single whole took on a revised direction — the USA, West Africa, Madrid, Marseilles, Liverpool. And so it must have been for many others like me dancing and singing in the band — this discovery that the stepping-off point to a full self was not so distant after all. We had a good time that day in 1945 for, in our minds, we were all pretty near heroes already. And it didn't matter that we had never fired a gun ourselves, nor seen our neighbours dead and wounded. We had such a good time being grand heroes that when Anthony came back two years later we had nothing left to cheer him, and although there was a function nothing much was made of it. I was not there to see, but I heard. Nothing much was made of it. After all, the town paper had carried no news of his adventures, we knew nothing of what he did while he was away. Some said he might not have left Trinidad at all, but that was never known for sure because Anthony came back far less accessible to our village monitors, as though that retreat already begun with the loss of Cleo had taken him far along an irreversible track — where he existed in and only for himself. He spoke hardly at all to anyone, particularly among the redfaces it became known, so it was impossible to find out truly where he had been, or what he had seen. But everyone could tell how he was, because that showed plainly all over him. 'Like a young boy with a man's tribulations,' Grandfather said. In any case, he was not a Yank, and whatever he had done in the war certainly couldn't amount to much even though at the function for his homecoming he had the stage all to himself — if you paid no attention to the rumours about the other two. 'Defected to the Germans,' some said. 'Hitler killed those two fools,' others, or others yet, 'They're still sweeping the streets of England.' In any case they had not returned, and not many of us cared, because, we had from the beginning understood some calamity inevitably had to befall them. Anthony had the stage to himself, but all those who had come to the function hoping to hear him relate an adventure or two — the capturing of a German town, the rescue of a Belgian princess, perhaps — were disappointed. Anthony sat aloof. Old redface, the father, thanked God for the safe return of his son, and praised the village for what he called our extraordinary war effort, but the boy, stiff as a statue in his double-breasted khaki uniform with its brass trimmings, said not a word. And when time came for everybody to stand and sing 'God save the king' they did, but it was a half-hearted effort.

125

And all this time I was already away, having made that preliminary shipless journey north to the orphan home — which would eventually land me on George Street — and the cockatoo psychiatrist whom I had never heard of before, but whose permission was necessary before I got the job. To be followed by the real journey as M. Shepard apprentice counsellor/teacher, and not the final ride of its kind either, because the City was an alien place that could not keep you out but took its time about letting you in. So for the first year, every fortnight a repetition of that shipless journey between village and City, and in the second year not every fortnight, but picking up each time a little hearing about Anthony — how he shunned the redfaces' club for the Chinese rumshop although he never spoke to anyone there, just sat and played with his bottle until it was empty; how he never said a word to Eccles when the two met along catwalks in the factory, nor a word to Cleo either, who sometimes when she brought Eccles' lunches to the gate would see Anthony and begin to raise a hand or smile then let either act suffer a quiet death because not even with his eyes did he acknowledge her. Hearing about him on my weekend returns to the village, and sometimes seeing him at a distance, remote behind the wheel of his Company jitney, the young noble head going gaunt. And the redfaces tried the same trick again, feeding him something native, but this time the results were off from those they wanted because it was Betty who grew more docile, whose eyes filled up with a peaceful smile, especially after both by word and appearance she announced in the manner of a public secret that she was carrying his child. For Anthony, not the least change — except as it were to become more gaunt, to advance from one bottle to two, to have fewer words for anyone, even the men he overseered — reducing his wishes to a series of simple signs, while becoming a village prop in a way no redface had ever been before. Turning up at village dances. Sitting with the workers at cricket matches. But never saying a word, unless some utterance was absolutely unavoidable, and sometimes not even then. 'A young boy with a man's tribulations,' Grandfather said. 'Why doesn't his father send him away?' A question asked by quite a few, because already the younger brother was gone — England to become a lawyer, some said, Canada to become a doctor, others, Australia, that's where he's gone, the most authoritative. Don't you know that's where these white folks settle after making their pile in the colonies? But wherever the young one was, the question remained, why did Anthony stay behind? Why did his father let him stay behind when the boy was so obviously withering away? Nobody knew, but there was much guessing about that too. Guessing about everything.

Black man you're a loser, and all the guessing in the world can't make a bit of difference about that.

Friday 11th, 11 o'clock

So who asked him to bring himself and those stupid little brats there? Was he teaching them anything about flags and ships? What a stupid thing to be doing — running around the Savannah in all that heat and humidity! Only a few minutes with my eyes closed under the linden shade, and already I am interrupted by this stupid schoolteacher and his silly girls, giggling and mixing their little legs into relay teams. First bend to the right, next to the left, then touch the toes, then one hup two hup again, like awkward young butterflies trying to fly but not being able to get off the ground. Whoever thought to dress little black girls in red overall skirts and white blouses, anyway? This teacher, so energetic! But clumsy. Short, with low hung paunch, he could only make half a bend himself, could run only as a sort of upright duck — heels first, and open palms swinging in the region of the waist. His white shirt soaked, plastered to his back, so that it was no longer white, but luminous black where the skin showed through. 'Hup, hup, hup! Run! Run!' the girls sending off giggles and screams in their high voices; not a thought for the towering flags above, nor the thousands of ships that over more time than was easily imagined had brought them here. I should have brought my boys to the Savannah. Incredible, that in all my three years at the orphan home I never once brought my boys to the Savannah for this kind of cavorting and twisting about. But why worry? Time has already passed, future days already forfeit. And though it might please the plump peacock of an Inspector to dawdle a month, six months, he might come next week or today, and whenever he comes I must be more than ready. Prepared for whatever their justice might prescribe — a hanging, or a dim cell. A hanging, dangled limply from the gibbet, not difficult to imagine that. The Indian looked as though some colossal accident had snapped him up by the neck. And if the criminal took too long to die, it was said, they slashed veins at the back of his legs and drained him. not too difficult to imagine it, but very difficult to escape the paralysis once the imagination gets started on hanging there in a noose, unable to control the loss of tongue, or keep a calm face. And on top of that to feel some attendant slashing, searching for veins, feel the bowels and bladder let go beyond any stopping. Or if not that, no hanging, shut away in some solitary cell with no one to see or hear, no one to touch. Locked up within four dark walls, talking to the brick cement, making friends with the bars. And with nothing left behind, either. No son to say, or think, 'He had style though.'

From the edge of the Savannah I watched the ungainly schoolteacher and envied the days he had ahead of him in the open air. I would never bring my boys out to exercise alongside his girls. I would never, as a matter of fact, see the orphan home again. It belonged to time already passed, and the future was forfeit. But was it?

Until finally the clouds did make their way over the hilltops, lumbered west intent on covering the sun, and with the first drops of the late afternoon rain I turned my back on the scampering, screaming girls and their teacher, and started back to George Street. With no hurry. No need to hurry. This rain might be the last I should ever feel so warm and explosive in the face. No need to hurry through undressing, and making a pot of tea; no need to hustle my letter to the director of the orphan home. Today was a long day.

And that would have been all right, except it kept adding, 'But not long enough. Not half long enough.' So after a while I had to go downstairs to The Undertaker. After I had circled around the possibilities of a brave finish, preened like a cockatoo, let my feathers down and preened again, and gnashed my beak a dozen times, I went downstairs to The Undertaker. Today was not a day to be tiptoeing around in my room: so I would go down to The Undertaker, take him in too, and finish off the need to be furtive. Today was my day. I would not have my privacy bothered by the obtrusive ears downstairs. Go down and make them mine. But before that, before I put that down in its proper place, there was the time when I visited the cockatoo psychiatrist. Which was a long time ago, before I met Hille, and I didn't know then that that's what he was until someone told me. That is, I knew about his being a cockatoo of course — his feathers and comb were all in clear sight — but didn't for a moment suspect him of being also the other, although I well might have. 'So your father is dead,' were his first words. 'Your mother too, in a practical sense. Stop talking in a monotone and tell me the truth about your dreams.'

'Aha ha ha!' he laughed. 'So true! So true is the pattern. Like picking grapes off a dead vine. So. Your sister turns you down and you are a frustrated man.' 'I have no sister.' 'Shut up! Your good true friend turns his ass in your face, has full advantage of the sister you wanted, and you are paralysed to think that one man could do that to another. To think! Do you hear me? To THINK!'

Then after I had accepted another invitation to speak he screamed, 'Stop your senseless chatter about consequences. Do you think you're the only one?' Circling the floor he preened, then suddenly like an insane harpy leaped in screeching, 'You are trapped. Above, guilt and hatred. Below, filth, disease, worms. Trapped, my friend. Contrary to what you believe, you are not a doctor-bird. You cannot hover in between. It's either up or down. That's good. We need people like you. Our task here is highly peculiar — you will understand when I tell you that here we undertake neither to clean nor correct. Do you understand? Neither clean nor correct. Filth is filth; boys are boys; people are people. All of it exists, none of it will ever change. We undertake here merely to cope with the existing and unchangeable, and the motif upon which our behaviour turns is stamina. Do you understand? Stamina! According to my diagnosis you are good for two years — more, if you manage to forget this Anthony and Cleo business. I recommend that the orphan home hire you. Do you want the job?'

Do you understand? Do you understand? What was there for me to understand, besides needing a job? And not in the footsteps of Grandfather. The fields were waiting, so too the factory — sticky syrup-covered rails and catwalks. Come into my parlour, said the spider to the fly. Fly in molasses. No fields. Factory neither. Not when you're educated. So what does an educated man do? Principally, creates others like himself. Drunks create drunks, robbers create robbers, labourers labourers, and educated men may not escape the principle. So, all right. Educated men also create fools. But that's merely an inescapable by-product, not the real thing. Like our river which ran the stink off from the sugar factory. So after the Reverend-tutor, and my time at the high school, seeing as I qualified for the term educated, there was nothing left for it but to spread the germ. And why choose an orphan home? For that I cannot account, except in those days I did have some vague notion of following in the tutor's steps. Too, there was the occasion to travel. From my village to the City, a handsome fifty miles. None of it by ship, but that did not matter. There would be enough ships in the harbour at Port-of-Spain, with smells and colours from every corner of the world. A handsome fifty miles, without ship, but so much nearer to ships. And, besides, Anthony was gone, but there was no going to war for me.

So proud was Grandfather! Here then a drop of his blood dressed in suit and tie, destined for a gentleman's career. Refined. And Cleo came to cry goodbye, even though I had seen her only from a distance since the night of the Italian wine. She came to cry goodbye — before all the old women of the village, who sat with their dresses pulled low in their laps remembering what quite a hand they had in raising me, in saving me from the devil and destruction — and to murmur how deeply she hoped to see me again, even though it was understood that I should be back each fortnight to bring Grandfather 'something' and pick up clean washing. So, onward fifty miles to the cockatoo psychiatrist who only afterwards someone said what he was, who demanded to know my life story — as though I would ever tell it, even if I could — whose conclusive diagnosis ran that with my fixation on Betty — bitch and sister — my frustrated wish to be like Anthony — which caused me to identify with him yet desire his death — I was excellent material. Of what other to fashion workers of the filth-muck bottom floor of the universe? And somewhere intuitively I must have understood that he was no different, was too after creating others in the likeness of his own image; intuitively understood that cockatoo was the by-product of some educated man, and that it was not given I should suffer in the image of his likeness. Thanks for the job. 'Psychiatrists always have more questions than they have answers,' Hille later told me, 'and it's seldom that you find one who knows what he's talking about.' That kept me very proud of the way in which I had dealt with cockatoo.

The Undertaker was a different business. He had a soothing voice, despite the range it covered, and I thought, what else? On the whole one must expect them to have soothing voices. Sometimes he was in high C, then suddenly into middle F, but always soothing. A protean voice, like his face, remarkable for fitting any highlight any moment, but in fact without any highlights of its own. It could have been his voice, not mine, telling, ' . . . but aren't village funerals stupid affairs though! All the crying, and singing. You know, when my father was buried, I kept wishing they would all stay home. The women with their big skirts, and their loud voices, hugging their bellies and moaning as though it was part of themselves going to be buried. I felt like crying too, but with all that wailing going on around me I couldn't. I listened to the music instead. The same music as we would have had for a Society marching. I suppose because he was a musician and a lodge member too. "Onward Christian soldiers", the same music. So I followed behind the hearse thinking, this is really a marching, not a funeral; and if there weren't all these women mewling from their bellies it could have been just like a marching too. Ended up like one, with the men crowding their black suits into the rumshop, and the women putting off changing their white Sunday dresses until bedtime. But the crying spoiled it.' 'So you would have a funeral without crying? Listen, the only place I have seen such a funeral is in New York. No hollering, not a tear, not a hat on lopsided, everything in its place. Perfect. Everything moving like clockwork. And what a casket! None of the cheap stuff we make down here — a walnut finish, and purfled edges, and twisted gold handles. If only I could get caskets like that for my shop! Now that was a funeral — stylish, and steady as clockwork. I don't even bother going to ours since I saw that one.' 'I didn't realise you had been to New York.' 'How could you? Where a man's been doesn't have to show on his face.' 'Other places too? Besides New York.' 'Not first class ones. Just Boston and Philadelphia and Chicago.' 'How do people walk in those places?' 'Walk? Oh, you think they walk a different way every place you go? Well, they do and they don't. They hurry more. They're always in a hurry. And most of the time they don't see where they're going. But that's not particularly different.' Could have been his voice all the way. 'The same as people walk here? Even down to where they put their eyes?' 'The same. Except here you can see a body squinting up against the sun while over there everybody wears big glasses so you don't see any eyes at all. Will you have some tea?' Yes of course I would have some tea, and listen to the voice ' . . . doesn't she come from New York? Somebody told me she was American.' Not from New York. Indiana. 'Does she like Benny Goodman?' Who? 'Benny Goodman.' Oh. She never said anything about him. 'But man, you are supposed to find out what your lady friend likes.' Without a record-player? I don't have one. 'Can't you get one? I know where you can get one for next to nothing. Or you can borrow mine . . . ' Hille loves her country. That's what she loves. She said so herself one day after she asked, 'Don't you love Trinidad?' A silly question which I didn't bother answering. 'You must love it,' she insisted. 'The land, the people, the atmosphere, they are all uniquely yours, and you just as uniquely belong to them. Besides, how can you love someone else if you don't love your country? How can you be amiable with yourself? You can't love me until you've started liking yourself.' Then out of spite I had to ask, 'Do you love your country?' 'Of course!' she came back, nonchalant but biting, the way she lets you know she is not among the misguided. 'Of course! Since I was a child. I love the plains. I remember days there when the sky was so blue it was almost piercing. And the fields! Field after field of wheat and ripe corn. You could see the wind on them, rippling the stalks like a giant invisible hand, feel it measure you from head to toe beneath whatever you're wearing, a bold yet discreet caress. That's how I like to be touched. In autumn, you could smell richness in the air. Sometimes, when I was a girl, I used to lie in the woods and let the crisp red and brown leaves flutter down on my face. I used to wear a thin dress so that wherever they landed on me I could feel the soft bump of their edges. I've always loved my country in the autumn. In the springtime too. One spring, before I went to college, father took me to the

133

mountains. I had never gone before and I had butterflies in my stomach all the way. When I first saw the mountains in the distance they looked so soft, so blue and feminine, I remember wishing they were mine; wishing in a child's way that all those soft pointed things were growing out of my body. But when we got to them the mountains were rough, scrubby, with lots of rocks. I was disappointed, until we got to the very top where there was still snow on the ground between the pine trees. What a glorious cleanness! We walked in the snow, and all around the green trees and white ground sparkled with golden sunshine under the blue sky. I had never been in such a quiet place before in all my life. I felt like I was growing. Then father walked me to the edge of the slope, warning me not to look down. I looked down anyway, and my breath stopped. It was like standing on the edge of the world. I could almost feel the earth spinning. And down below, stretching all the way to the horizon, field after field, green and growing. There was life and richness in the air, and a sense of power — just as if everything I saw belonged to me. Even the sky. On the way home I looked back again, and the mountains were just as they were when I first saw them — tall, blue, soft against the sky. And I wished all over again that they were growing out of me. But I was destined to be flat-chested, ha ha . . . ' What nonsense. What complete nonsense listening to her, and unable to stop myself saying, 'But no moonlight, eh?' Moonlight, but nothing like ours — that's what she said. My saying didn't stop her a bit from going on though, 'Haven't you ever felt anything like that for Trinidad? Don't you love your country? I'm really proud of mine — especially now we are leaders of the free world.' Warriors. Iwo Jima, Guadalcanal. In my ear the echo of '*Onward Christian soldiers, marching as to war*', my people strutting, enjoying themselves. Yes, onward. Onward where to? To the church. And after there, to the lodge building for a banquet. Onward indeed. How beaten and ragged, how puny they looked, these marchers, coming home from their marching weary of behaving in a manner befitting their Sunday dress; weary and stuffed and telling others what a good time; mothers and aunts bringing away snacks in their handkerchiefs for their young ones. 'My feets hurt.' How weary they looked, how ludicrous, in the feathered hats sweat-slobbed, and the men, waking up the Chinese rumseller from his Sunday afternoon nap, sneaking in through the back of the store to put the cap on the occasion of their black serge suits, crediting like fiends towards, into, a drunk, albeit today in the style of gentlemens, with all high diction flying, quotations in the Latin and memories of erudite historical facts. 'When was Queen Victoria's birthday?' 'Who settled South Africa?' 'How many years did the Boer's war last?' 'What day did Edward abdicate?' 'What was the Belgian national anthem in the First World War? And the French? And the English? *God save the King. Rule Britannia, Britannia rules the waves, Britons never never never shall be slaves* . . . ' What voices! In a moment of high drunk camaraderie, what voices! Then back to '*Onward Christian soldiers*' in four parts, the black ties hung low, the starch-stiff collars now softened under the constant flow of sweat down the face and neck, sweat coursing down into the dinged shirts no longer white. Grey is the colour of my father's chest! '*To be or not to be, that is the question.*' Who wrote that? And off again, a gallop of voices in a rum stink, sweat-drenched room, with the Chinaman patiently serving another one and adding figures in his dog-eared ledger. Until the sun sinks out of sight, and as if wary of travelling in the night they stagger out into the momentary dusk intending to hurry home, shoes slung around the shoulder, serge coats dragging in the dirt, collars flopping by their well worn studs. '*Sans eyes, sans teeth, sans hair.*' Who wrote that? Sans everything really, except a high drunken spirit against sadness, nurtured down the road, and into the house until sleep came. In my ear the echo of those voices — '*Onward Christian soldiers,*' and the slap of weary feet down the dusty road, punctuating a song that had lost its power; the echo of a drunken mysticism that could not be

135

let down for a single moment if Sunday would be any different from Monday in the fields, if Sunday were to be any respite of unthinking about the fields. So Christian soldiers. That was what I had to love. Growing up unloving and frightened, but not knowing why. I see it now. Christian soldiers without understanding what soldiering was. Without understanding what this Christian Church was. 'Who discovered the New World?' 'Columbus.' Very proud. They taught me that in school. Yet no one thought to emphasize that without the Christian church Columbus might never have come West, he nor the redfaced overseers who rode the village. They might never have come West, but they did, with the blessings of the Christian church. The New World was discovered for the European. I had to remember that. America was not discovered for me. On the contrary, I was discovered for it. Which discovery took place when some smart christianized businessman happened upon a source of black cargo along the Guinea Coast and awakened his brother Christian soldiers to that vast reservoir of sweat and blood just ready to be piped across the Atlantic for to soak down and soften the new wilderness land. Onward Christian soldiers through the two o'clock village heat, sweating under the satin banners, the rosettes and regalias, marching behind a band out of tune from lodge to church, later staggering from rumshop to home, sans even a council of war. How be proud of a people who played at fighting for heaven on earth, who felt in the name of heaven was a foregone winner and therefore saw fit to be assured of a mystical victory while never fighting for an actual one? Of course, in those days I never could have said this to myself. I looked forward then to being a marcher too, with the gayest rosette of all pinned to my lapel, until Hille came along, and somehow it seemed wrong when she saw so much to love and be proud of in my village. Was his voice, 'Yes, I know what you mean. Once they start loving they love everything, from man to cockroach without distinction. And they could do that easily, you know, because neither cockroach nor man is a match for the superman. But you have to expect that. You shouldn't let it worry you too much. Every black man born in the New World has to pass through that same bitterness whether he recognizes it or not. Best to get it over with quick as you can.' Still his voice after a short silence, 'So she loves her country, eh? But that doesn't tell you whether she likes Benny Goodman or not. There is something you should know! What kind of flowers does she like? See! You never even brought one to her. Did you ever take her on a boat ride down to Los Cottoros? Never? Now that's the sort of thing you want to be doing. She's still a woman, you know.' Yes, still a woman. Would have continued saying so too were there not some strange relationship between her and the stubborn redface whom she had never before seen, about whom she knew only what I told her, but who in an instant became some kind of instinctual brother. Anthony, whom his father had wanted to go away, it was known in the village, his brother having gone — to become a lawyer, some said, and spend the rest of his days making speeches in Parliament. The mother was gone too, for finally the tropic heat had drained her dry and refilled her with nothing but fever. Those who saw her leave said she looked like a withered ghost, and this was good for the pride of the villagers who had spent, were spending, their lives taking the best the god-damned sun could offer in and around the white man's fields. But Anthony would not budge. It seemed he had no regard for the fortune which it was rumoured remained his, back across the water, even though some malady was draining him down so the noble features, the military chest brought back from the war, were all sunken in. I used to see him on my Sundays in the village, flashing past in the green jitney, his bony fingers clamped to the wheel, his face like a pale mask fixed forward, neither left nor right. And it was not the same as in the past when his father, the Overseer, had rocketed down our road scattering chickens and dogs, scattering my friends and I from our marble game. The Overseer had thick hands and a plump face, and there was nothing anybody in the world could do for him. He was a man so assured his wheels had most right to be where he put them, he swerved aside for no one. Anthony was different. The boys playing marbles or cricket in the road would stand aside to let him pass, but if one happened to be slow getting out of the way the jitney would whip sharply around and whip back again to dodge whoever he might be, and go on whipping left and right until everyone was safe in the dust. The bravest boys were always deliberately slow in taking their bottoms out of Anthony's way, and each time he went through his frenzied swerving to avoid hitting them a great laugh went up from the whole gang. It was my duty to warn them against playing with their lives, but secretly I laughed with them. I used to see him, but he never saw me, and things were back as though we never had ridden together. Oh yes, we rode our bikes together from the high school. Had to, to protect ourselves from the town boys until he became a face riding in the back of his father's Company car. I never let the boys see me laughing openly though. Amazing how that sort of thing gets into the blood — I felt guilty. Sunday after Sunday, the same incident, the same results — the boys' laughter and mine, and feeling guilty. Until one Sunday when practically everyone from the village, and many redfaces too were packed in for the last cricket match of the season. The same pavilion where once I had crawled away from my gambler friend and his girl, retching in the dark. The Company, you know, always put up a challenge cup for competition among its employees, their friends and relatives. A gala occasion, this final match of the season, with the redfaces out in full numbers, cramped in the boxed enclosure always reserved for them; not least among them this day the manager's wife, wearing her native pink frock, postured like a long-beaked bird guarding the six inch challenge cup on its pedestal beside her. After the match she would offer her hand to the winning captain, inclining ever so gracefully as she grinned while presenting him the cup. She and the others — all the men shirt-sleeved in fine linen —

138

seated in unnatural grace, affecting a superior interest barely this side of boredom, much in the style which fine gentry must have affected for the lists during the reign of Ivanhoe. Anthony was at the match too, but he did not sit among them. He had a seat apart, somewhere between the redfaces and the villagers, and there was a visible space all around him. I was there — that same pavilion in which I had crawled away on hands and knees — Betty and Stone were there, and Cleo, and Eccles; and when I think about it now I could see us like five little islands in that raucous rowdy pavilion, caught up in our separate destinies that had nothing to do with which team won the cup. Eccles, shirt-sleeved among the gentry, Cleo some distance down beneath him, and between them Anthony. Myself to the right, slightly behind Anthony, and beneath me Stone and Betty, and all around us the field men, the factory workers — Indians, Africans, and Trinidad's own special duglas. From Palmyra the visiting team came that Sunday bringing with them a bowler named Ragoo who always delivered hard and fast; a bowler destined to cause trouble at a match in which team rivalry had already run over into vocal hostility between the visitors and locals. Ragoo's bumpers would hit you in the stomach before you could think, and it was obvious the only reason our village batsman suffered through the first innings without too many complaints to the umpires, or an outright attack upon Ragoo himself, was the sight of that six inch cup gleaming on its pedestal beside the manager's wife. Although I wasn't paying much attention. For me the match was strictly a way of killing time until my bus arrived, when I would gather up my change of clothes and catch it back to the City, and George Street, where Hille should be waiting. A way of killing time, an occasion for watching too, in that special way I had learned to watch since leaving the village — as though they were all real, but I a reflection of my real self ensconced in a remote place, the me in sight not the real thing at all, but a sort of reflection. Do you understand what I mean? Well, then, I was watching, hostile at

Eccles, and feeling a little pity for the solitary state in which Anthony sat. And Cleo too. [Let me finish, and then I'll tell you who all these people are. They're just village people, my village people.] Cleo sitting by herself too, although there were three of us — or just two of them — with whom she had been at one time or another joined man-woman. Irrelevant really, that it was a close match; so close that four runs in the last over would make all the difference — one of those storybook games. Like five separate islands we sat — I can't speak for the man Eccles, having not known him except from a distance as an enemy whose bones I would myself smash should fortune provide the chance — seemingly, except for Stone and Betty, with no connection between us. Even with the crowd getting to its feet in the last over. I stood up too, with my bag of clean clothes in my hands, and I could see Anthony clearly, although he didn't stand up. The khaki uniform he always wore since he came back from the war was rough done and splotched down the back as he hunched over puffing on a cigarette. And, yes, we had not exchanged a single word since he came back, but I still felt pity for that singleness in which he sat with the empty spaces all around him. Moments with Cleo — they came to mind (No, she didn't look back once, or make any sign that she had seen me) and I couldn't help thinking about the bare white servant room with its narrow metal bed that held the door from opening fully, the chest-of-drawers, metal too, tall and narrow with the chalky mirror above it, (Yes. At Anthony's father's house] the one swinging light, long on a cord from the ceiling, black cord as long as the gentle pendulum motion of the bulb was not disturbed to send flies buzzing about the room. Cleo, slightly damp under the arms, and hot breasts loose beneath the maid's uniform, a hand for Anthony, one for me (Yes, each hand) and he with a narrow serious face beneath his pale hair innocent and yet intense, and eyes that had not yet gone to seeing nothing. In imitation of the father, I suppose. In those days, when we were both captivated by the mystery beneath

Cleo's skirts, the one I should have imitated was a wanderer, off pleasing women in strange villages. Cleo did everything in style when style was at her disposal, and that afternoon while Anthony sat in circumscribed isolation, not three rows away, she stood the finest of the village fine on a Sunday afternoon — fuschia dress, that even from a distance set a man's senses grinding on dreams of mystery and stupefaction in the dark, (No, the American girl doesn't have much mystery. She isn't interested in that sort of thing) arms akimbo, slender black arms, and hands not fine, but expressive. Hands that led Anthony into the world, and me too, somewhat. Hands that could not only lead but cajole, denounce to the regions of hell. Go to hell Ragoo! You think you doin something with your bumpers? We gon win this match! With a fist and a finger. And not only a red dress and black hands, but a candy coloured hat, and a striped parasol that for the moment lay between her feet. 'Go to hell Ragoo,' and she was part of a big chorus which included Stone and Betty her sister too; Mr Stone who now had his own billiard parlour and cafe, or who, it was said, ran Betty's billiard parlour and cafe, the same everyone knew belonged to Anthony really but never spoke that out except in whispers. Cleo's dress and parasol probably came from Eccles, but Anthony owned Betty — her dress, her parasol, her hat — and whatever treatment from her hands money could buy. But he didn't own the hands though, nor the rest of the body his dress covered, except perhaps the slight bulging around the waist which Betty said was his child. Come, pay for your fun, and when that's over let's have done until the next time — even though she made no visible difference in his dealings with his father and the other redfaces, and they thought feeding her to him had been a failure. The grandfathers and everyone else in the village knew Anthony was keeping Betty, (Yes, she used to work for his father, but she quit after the mother went back to England) that he probably threw on her more money than most of them would bring home in a lifetime. They laughed at him, were jealous, and called him a fool, and passed on the news with a surreptitious smirk whenever Betty accorded them the pleasure of taking their few shillings in the dark. Betty did things in her own style. And while Anthony was her keeper, the grandfathers and others her customers, Stone was her gentleman. Decked out in brand new flannel pants and Hawaiian silk shirt, he too was on his feet beside her shouting in caustic voice, 'Ragoo go home. This match is ours!' Betty nor Stone, neither had eyes for Anthony, and I, so intently focusing my pity upon his humped figure missed the climactic instant of the game. I recognized that when the crowd's roar changed to a howl of anger, and I felt the press of hands and bodies against my back propelling me down towards the field. I dared not miss my bus. It was the last until dawn of Monday morning. I fought to hold my ground, but it was hopeless. In a rush I was taken past the row in which Anthony sat, down amidst a tangle of sweaty limbs and bodies, until I too was forced to brace myself against the back before me. And on the green grass field one of our village batsmen was after Ragoo. As the tumble of angry voices kept bearing down, I saw him chase after Ragoo paddling the air with his bat, and Ragoo too trying to escape, but not fast enough. The batsman caught up and smacked the willow against his head, and Ragoo went down. His team-mates jumped on the batsman, and he went down. Our village team was upon the visitors, and the crowd was upon all of the players, and I was trying to disentangle myself from among them and not lose my bag of clean clothes. Most of the crowd couldn't get to where the fighting really was, so in the rush many fights broke out, even among friends. I had to throw a few blows too to keep from going down. Turned around, facing the pavilion where I sat two minutes ago, I found myself standing over the bleeding Ragoo. Blood trickled from his nose and ears, and thick red foam oozed from the corner of his mouth. Many were kicking him still, and I wanted to reach down and cover him up. And I like to tell myself I would have rescued Ragoo if it wasn't time for my bus to be at the junction, time for me to be on my way back to Hille. (Yes. That's her name. Her father owns oilships) I had to go. But suddenly I heard a voice I half knew, 'Cut him up, cut him up,' and when I looked around this Indian from our village — who always called himself Son of the Prince of Punjab — was waving a cutlass overhead. The blade was clean and shiny as though he had been sanding it for years. 'Cut him up,' that was Betty, beside me, her nostrils quivering, and I remembered how Cleo used to look like an excited horse. Then silence. Coming swiftly from the outer edges of the crowd around Ragoo, as though some voice-sucking spirit came bristling through, and when it arrived upon the body of Ragoo it was none other than Anthony. 'Clear out,' in a voice just like the Inspector's when he orders his policemen about. (Oh yes. I know the Inspector. We know each other quite well. As a matter of fact he'll probably be along for a visit some time soon) 'Clear out,' and all the robust villagers allowed themselves to be moved aside by his skinny arms. Even the Son of the Prince of Punjab let fall his weapon arm, and Anthony, the pale hair spilling over his forehead, came forward with his eyes focused upon the prostrate Ragoo. 'Clear out, clear out' he kept saying, pressing the crowd back with his arms. Suddenly, behind him and the crowd of muttering black faces, above the manager's wife who stood beside the challenge cup with one red hand to her mouth, beyond the last rows of the pavilion I saw the red and yellow bus that should take me back to Hille, nudging itself slowly through the mob spilled backwards across the road. My escape. No other bus to Hille until dawn. I had nothing to do with Ragoo, nor the others who hemmed me in on either side, so that when Anthony's arm fell against my chest, a sudden fury in my throat, and I knocked it away. Knocked him stumbling backwards for a foot or two. But he was quick. Before I could recall my eyes a second time from the indifferent bus he struck back. I felt his bony fist against my face, and groped to regain my balance. I raised my bag, but in the meantime his fists had struck several times, and

sooner than I could tell what was doing I fell down beside
Ragoo. To my knees first, then I lay down. Mine was the only
hand raised against Anthony that day. From where I was trying
to get up off the turf I saw him hoist Ragoo to his shoulders
then start back towards the steps of the pavilion out the very
lane he had made coming in through the crowd. And as shock
waves of silence had preceded him in, so a clatter of voices —
as though awakening suddenly from paralysis — arose behind
his footsteps as he made his way out with Ragoo's blood joining
the sweat down the back of his shirt. (No. He didn't do much
damage. My face was puffed up a little, but that was all) My
bus was gone. The villagers busily trailing their rage after
Anthony and Ragoo, or seeking out the other Palmyra players
had no attention to spare for me. I gathered up my clothes, and
picked myself up off the grass. I was not losing blood. None of
my blood trickled down my chin. Instead it passed through my
veins like hot needles, and although I had not gone to war, been
trained in the art of killing, Anthony was to die there and then.
I jumped into the crowd, but lost the khakied figure with its
burden. Our constable at the head of the steps was trying to part
a way through for the manager's wife; but he was old, had no
venom for dealing with his neighbours, and many villagers who
normally would have effaced themselves and given a rod to the
wife where she needed a foot brushed past her irreverently in
pursuit of the Palmyrians. Most of the visiting players had
already managed to climb onto their lorry, and from there were
defending themselves with bats and stumps. The challenge cup
had fallen from its pedestal, and the redfaces, at last joining
hands, attacked the mob as a unit, making a way for themselves.
Then I was so close to Anthony once more, I could have charged
and bowled him over from behind, but I didn't. I followed, and
watched him place the injured bowler in the rear of his jitney
then climb in the cab himself, all this time his face unchanged —
pale eyes focused into some realm he alone saw, peeled lips
tight, though neither threatening nor compassionate. I watched

144

everything he did — this man everyone said had come back from the war loaded with killer's blood — and as I watched his stooped shoulders drive away I knew his blood, war or no war, could be no deadlier than mine — for the prickling hot streaks that made sweat come fast and cold around my forehead shrieked one command, kill! kill! and I don't know why I was waiting, or what for. I did not kill Anthony that night. I did not kill anyone that night — except, perhaps, myself a little. Soon after the jitney drove off it became dark, and I followed the stragglers back into the village proper where they congregated mostly beneath the rumshop eaves. I walked on and sat by myself in front of the billiard parlour now owned by Betty and Stone. Closed on Sundays. In the coming dark I began feeling like a stranger in the village. Stranded, and wanting very much not to be there. Fleeting wishes that the bus would somehow come back and take me away to George Street and Hille clashing with the pain where my jaw had gone stiff. After a while, not many people on the road. The Chinaman couldn't open his front door on Sundays, but I could hear some drinkers he had let in through the back of his shop still wrapped up in the fighting. Those who had blood stains on their clothes yelling about it. Hardly a sound in the village besides that though, until an early dog howled and the church bell started ringing for the evening service. The stars were already coming out and past the factory and pond lights were coming on too to spot the houses where the redfaces lived. Once in the past, on Sunday night after the game, I would at this time be getting ready for evening service — shined shoes, hymn book, collection money, and in my heart a suppressed fluttering for Cleo who would be waiting on her bed beneath the hanging bulb. I outsmarted Grandfather on those nights — particularly when he was too drunk to remember what time I came in. (Well, it wasn't the redfaces so much, he didn't want me to have anything to do with them, that's true, but it was mostly women. If he had found out I was playing with a woman, he might have put me out) I outsmarted

145

Cleo, and my then compère Anthony too. For while I never groaned in mimic of a grown man the way he did, (His father, he said. He used to listen to the old man with his mother) I had my designs for the day when I should make (Yes, I had heard it lots of times at the tutor's) Cleo cry like the woman she was. No grapes and apples and wine. I would make her cry, (No. He wasn't a real tutor. I just call him that because he got me started on reading a lot of books I never would have known existed otherwise. He was a reverend. Who didn't believe in superstitions) make her cry just like the woman she was. That sweet crying which I could tell what it was from my own imagination. But in those days I was a child, and triumph lay in concealing all the plots and designs I didn't quite know how to fulfil. Quite a lot's happened since then. Grandfather, diminished by time, wrung dry by the scorching vituperative days, sat dominated by his chair. Still the open Bible on his lap, the nip bottle on the floor beside him, but mostly his eyes closed, chin sunk down on his dry chest as he dozed. And on the Sunday occasions when he stirred to welcome me and gloat for a few moments on his pride and joy — the boy he had reared with his own hands, according to his own rules, whose destiny he had indomitably tied to a book of truth for all black men — it was a mystery then why I ever had to outwit the bleary bloodshot eyes, the trembling mouth, this bald black head with its halo of tufted grey hair, this composite that was so convinced of its fantasies that had nothing to do with me at all. Yes, he harped on that from the first day he moved me into his house: Black man needs a book of truth about himself. His history. Looking at me all the time with his eyes saying 'maybe you?' And after I had promised (Yes, I promised. One of those emotional things. It was the night before I left on my big journey north, and with Cleo and all the other old women sitting there he comes out bigger than anything with 'My boy's going up north, but that's only the beginning. Don't lose your eyesight too soon, that way you'll miss the book he's going to

146

write about me and you and all us black people.' and the women all oooaahed and asked, 'Is you boy? Is you really goin' write a book about me and your grandpappy and all us people here in the village?' I had to say yes, with Cleo lighting up one of her big white smiles, saying nothing, but looking at me as though she knew what a secure place she already held in this book to be written. I said yes. That's all it takes to make a promise) and when Grandfather came so he was about to lose his eyesight and one or two other things beside, I had to keep telling him that the book was in writing and it won't be long before he can read it. A mystery it was, yet one not as great as why, since my bonds to the old man and the village had been so clearly ruptured, I still continued in my devious ways. Clearly, nothing had happened since the days of my childhood deceits, my adolescent triumphs. For instance, I knew very well how to settle the fury which stretched me like a snap-band between my stiff swollen jaw on one end and the yellow-red bus which as I sat would have had me more than half way back to Hille. And that was another rack, from the stone step of Anthony's-Betty's billiard parlour to Hille in my room on George Street, but not so hurtful as the first. I knew very well what to do. Some distance east from the cacophonous rumshop, the houses where the redfaces lived around the pond held many bright windows up to the night. Shut them. Make them dark. Shut every window around that pond, return the darkness to itself and breathe easier, then calmly lie down and wait for dawn to come up with its true light, and the first bus back to Hille. Yet, in spite of what I knew, I sat on Stone's step wondering, how would Anthony fare in the total dark? Would he recognize the implacable fury of blackness and lie down, or would he with his war training stand guard, beside his jitney perhaps, with its funnel beams playing at putting darkness to flight? No need to wonder, guess, at what he would do. I knew. There was a dance in the village that night, an after-game dance. And only after I heard the first music I realized how long I had been sitting. The musicians would never strike up before church was over. The last drunk had already staggered out the alley from behind the rumshop, and I had heard the Chinaman padlocking his gate. The honky sound of the dance band came softly down from the school-house, and by then I had sat long enough on Stone's step to be ready for what escape could be found in the village. The smell of rum and ice cream, laughing voices, pretty dresses, and above all dancing — giddy feet, a shallow dip of the hip and jerking waist — came back from last year, and the year before, and it was still sad, but not heartbreaking that the bus had left me behind. I had sat long enough, and in the meantime Anthony had gone by twice — once, I suspected, on his way from Ragoo's village, and once away from where the redface houses clustered around the pond. And both times his funnel beams came barrel-ling out of the night, he and his jitney ripping by with a roar, raising a clatter of dust behind. I could hear him coming from afar, for there was no other jitney like his in all the village, and neither time did I fulfil the wish to leap out into his bright lights, dance him off the road. Nor did I throw rocks, or send curses after him. I sat and watched him go by twice, each time with the darkness wrapped tight around his lights and the tumble of his aggressive engine dying into a distant moan, leaving the night once again to the dogs, some scolding mother, a crying child. Village voices. The honky dance band; but before that, distant voices harmonized in sweet lament from the church. And at times I sang a phrase or two with them because I knew the airs and words to every hymn they raised. And even after church was over, and the grandmothers in their shawls had gone by, pocking home in their square-heeled shoes, the music they had helped make at the church still hovered in the air, coming back again behind Anthony's mechanical rumble, coming back, linger-ing like a melodic echo about the village even after the dance band struck up, lifting a melancholy echo behind the bright brass.

I made my way to the dance hall, and it was all there. The schoolhouse was for that night converted into a minor circus of bright lights, gay sweaty faces, pretty dresses churning and jerking. The ice cream and rum smell was there, and many villagers all whom I knew, but none whom I could any longer honestly call friends. Dancers, and non-dancers, and slick ones with hats low over their eyes, shirt collars turned up in the latest style. Dresses and shirts and heaving bodies sending a hot smell through the windows, master-minded by the little band that raised enough music to intoxicate the whole village, And in the dark, drawn up against the school building was Anthony's jitney, with the hunched driver smoking over the wheel. Inside the hall, Betty chief among the wigglers, hat and umbrella for the time being stashed, red dress too tight to flare, mixing it up with Stone twist for turn, dip wiggle jerk, while the young master waited outside. Stone, flashing gold from cheek to cheek, far from least among the dancers, had his immaculate flannel pants belted low and his silk shirt opened flowing down to the navel. The grandfathers along the wall clapped and encouraged Betty and Stone lower deeper faster, from one end of the room to the other, recklessly between the other dancers, as though the music was playing only for them. And outside, Anthony waited. The boys who were too young to go in sat on his fenders, or dangled their legs from the tray of his jitney, while he sat gazing in, not even as close as I was, through the open window. And here was another chance for ambush, another chance to wipe out that sore spot on my face. The boom drum vibrating in my stomach, the trumpet screaming and trombone calling 'blood', called out 'blood', demanded some declaration, some commitment — the motive power of blood. White man can't dance! White man sit outside and wait, leave himself open for bottle or stone. Yet all the time, I had to be afraid, ashamed of myself too, for broken bottle and rocks can neither tell the story nor end it. I was afraid, but the dance called, and leaving my bundle of clothes beneath the window I strutted over to the jitney and jumped on his hood. The children scattered, and then laughed. But for all the reaction he showed, Anthony never saw me nor recognized the threat. I hit the hood again, and when he didn't move, I walked around to the driver's side and kicked the door. He pulled his eyes off Betty through the window then and gave the flicker of a smile before his face went blank again and he returned to staring. The dance called. 'Waiting for your woman?' I said. 'Why don't you go home? You went to war and you can fight — you know anything about how to dance?' The second glance he sent then said he wished but to be left alone. I knew he had sorrows on the inside. I had a sore spot on the face. But tonight Anthony and his sorrows belonged not here beside the schoolroom where the music was elemental and created for black faces. I snatched open the door of the jitney. 'Get out,' I said. 'Get out.' The boys gathered around. Anthony did not move. 'He crazy!' a young voice crackled behind me, and perhaps I was. The next instant my hands were wrapped in Anthony's collar, but he was firmly wedged in the seat and I couldn't move him. He swore and somehow managed to hit me again right on my swollen face, and this time I could feel the blood start. I reached up to touch it, perhaps stop it, and in that moment when I staggered back Anthony slammed the door, cranked his engine, and pulled off into the night. (Yes. He hit me twice in the same day, and the second time there was blood. I don't know if that meant anything to him) After the jitney was gone I found myself the centre of a noisy mob, mostly people who had come rushing from the dance hall at the children's cries. 'The white man hit him! The white man hit him!' And one of the peering grandfathers said 'That's Shepard's boy. I always said those two would come to blows.' The blood coming down my cheek, dripping dark spots on to my shirt, and I had some of it on my fingers. Many voices were talking, urging the boys to relate again and again what had happened, but no one came to see if I was deeply wounded. Neither did I care whether I was deeply

150

wounded. I wiped my fingers across my shirt, then unbuttoning it all the way down to the navel started for the dance hall. I pulled the hat low down on my forehead, and paid my two shillings at the door. The band was still playing, but the dancers paused to let me through. I might have been some sort of apparition newly arisen from the way they looked at me; but I was concerned with one only. The red dress was not hard to find. I made a path to Betty, cut her off from Stone, and he at first seemed ready to start a fight, but his eyes when he saw me fully lost it. When I grasped Betty's hand and put an arm about her waist Stone retreated, and I saw no more of him that night. She frowned. 'What you doing?' she said. 'Don't get your blood on me!' But the blood from my fingers was already upon her, getting lost in the redness of her dress, and though she was stiff, slightly resistant at first, I swung her around and shook her, forced her backwards until her arm found my waist; then the dancers gave us room, and by the time we were in the brightest spot beneath the musicians we had unison. Dance, Betty. Dance! Tonight you are in my hands, not me in yours. Hear the music. Mash. Wiggle. Feel the shape of my leg between yours. Her eyes closed, and the breath from her flaring nostrils streaked hot against my open chest. We owned the music, the smell of rum and ice cream, and sweat. We owned the night. And each time the musicians seemed coming to the end of their piece we stomped harder and set the dance floor shaking. Those watching and clapping from around the walls joined in, and the musicians went off again. It was past the hour of intermission when they stopped. I led Betty out into the cool night. 'Where you going?' she asked. 'Nowhere'. I led her down the steps of the school house and into the dark road. 'You acting like a real madman tonight,' she said. 'Where you going? The dance isn't over yet.' Of course the dance was not over, and we were going nowhere. Betty was sweaty and hot, and so was I, and the dance between us was far from finished. We were going nowhere but to a quiet place, a secluded place where we could continue the dance

151

between us without the intrusion of clapping grandfathers and brass music. The music there would be all my own, and any that she herself could make. 'We going to catch cold,' she said. 'I'm wet.' 'Me too.' 'What do you want to do?' 'Let's go to your house,' I said. 'Already? The dance isn't over yet. I paid my two shillings and I intend to dance till morning.' 'I paid my two shillings too, but the least we can do is get out of these wet clothes.' She laughed. 'You got something to change?' 'Yes.' She tried to withdraw her hand. 'And what if Stone come home?' 'I'll take care of that.' I wouldn't release her hand. 'You not afraid, eh?' she laughed. 'Let's go to your house, all right?' 'All right,' she said at last. And were I able to see her face in the dark I might have caught a warning. There was warning in her voice, but the dance called. I drew her close. 'I have to get my hat,' she said. 'It's in the hall.' She went in to get her hat, and while I was finding my bundle of clothes where I had left it beneath the window I saw her inside surrounded by Stone and the grandfathers. Each had a hand out to touch her. A caress on the shoulders, a pat on the ass, and in their eyes dreams of the days when they used to dance all night and still race the sun to the fields come morning. Some clearly pleaded with her to stay, although Stone didn't seem to care much, but she having found her hat, flitted her way laughing gaily between the hands and came back out to me. We led off down the road, and as we left the dance hall with its chatter and lit up windows behind, the darkness seemed to open up, accept intimately the echoes of our feet. Her throbbing hand in mine, I knew tonight I would be held again, but not as before (Her sister. Her sister used to hold us — the white boy and me — one in each hand, but I never had her to myself) (Well, one time. Betty. But Stone was there and that wasn't to myself either. Besides, that night I got sick) with a touch that was shared by Anthony in those servant room days. Tonight, after many nights with Hille submitting, I was no longer a child. And if Anthony could have been there he would have known that too.

He would have known that though I had not gone away to the war, though I had not walked through fields of dying men, and seen women with bayonets stuck deep into their breasts, I too had grown. Reading, writing, and counting. And countless days with not much else to do but see the world grow smaller, feel my heart grow bigger, bold, daring enough to beat boldly in Betty's bed, and to its own music. I had not crossed fields of dying men, but the only difference that made was that my adventures still lay ahead. 'How come you decided to stay in the village tonight?' she said. 'You bewitched me,' I said. She laughed. 'You a funny man. Months now you pass me up and down in this village as though I wasn't existing, and now you want to stay with me tonight?' 'So? I've wanted to stay with you since the time you worked at the Reverend's.' 'But you was just a boy then.' 'And you?' 'Young and foolish myself, in those days.' 'You always had sweet hands though.' 'That must be sweet talk because how could you know?' She laughed. 'You not the same,' she said. 'Tonight you acting like a madman. What got into you?' 'Didn't I say I wanted to be with you?' 'Is that why you got blood all over your face and hands? You should know better than to fight Anthony — he can kill.' 'I can kill too.' She laughed. 'You have something for me?' she asked. 'Like what?' 'Well you can't expect to stay with me all night for nothing.' 'What do you want?' 'I'm goin' need a new dress, since you finished this one. I got it from Anthony too, but you put blood all over it.' 'Can't buy you any dress tonight,' I said. 'I know. But tomorrow? You're staying in the village tomorrow? We can go to town and you can buy me a new dress just like this one. Or you can give me the money if you like.' There was enough of the grandfathers in me so that I felt proud in having soiled Anthony's dress. That, and jealous too because Betty had been wearing his dress at all. And how could I buy her a dress? How could I buy her the score of dresses I would have liked to offer — enough dresses to make certain she would need no more from Anthony? Reading, writing and counting never paid enough to buy whores dresses. Further, my dreams of crossing the Gulf to the Mainland could hardly stand the loss of how many shillings it would take to buy a new dress. (Yes. I used to dream of crossing to the Mainland — still do — and Liverpool, and Cadiz, and Africa) (Yes. A backward sort of journey, or, I mean, a journey backwards) (You mean there is really nothing for me to find out on the Mainland?) (Yes, Well, even if people walk the same and talk the same and look the same, maybe I won't feel the same. You understand? Here I am, you know, waiting for the Inspector, and still I have the feeling of being incomplete. Going to be finished feeling far, far unfinished) But one does not refuse the dance, one goes in debt instead. 'You want a red dress like this one?' I asked. 'Mmmm hmmm.' 'Don't you think you'd look nicer in a yellow, or a green one?' 'I like those colours too, but red I love best of all.' 'Black. Don't you like black?' 'It's all right; but it don't do much for me.' 'I'd like to see you in all kinds of dresses — red, brown, black — you look good in everything.' 'I have a new brown one already. You'll buy me a red one?' 'Tomorrow morning we'll go to town, and if we can't find a red one there that you like, we'll go up north. We'll go everywhere until we find a red one you like.' 'You really talking like a man,' she said. 'Sounding ready to act like one too.' And after we had gone a little way in silence, 'You still wanting to buy me the dress?' she asked. 'Mmmmm hmmmm.' She squeezed my hand hard, but the dance had already begun to slow down within me, and for the first time I could feel the coolness of the night breeze coming in through my damp clothes. Betty led me down the dark road which I could walk with my eyes closed ever since the days I used to run barefoot through the village. We had no light save the far away stars. She led me past the front doors of her-Stone's-Anthony's billiard parlour, closed tight, and through the yard on to the wicker porch of her house. Inside she lit a lamp, and I sat my bundle in a corner. I was much cooler now, and worrying once more about having missed the bus. Wondering

154

about Hille, sad at having missed the night with her. The next bus was due at five, and even with that I would miss half a day's teaching, half a day's pay. Money. Passageway across the Gulf. Hille. A dusky shadow in the dark smelling nights. The blue Gulf. Grey sometimes, Hille and lavender. Hille naked and writhing. Her voice. Such a multitude of fretful thoughts, I did not see Betty undress, or perhaps her rustlings I had thought of as the unveiling of one more mysterious shadow in the room. It was a strange room, close, and light-absorbing, cluttered with things of indeterminate shapes — except the bed. The iron bedstead with brass adornments, spread out in white sheets as chilling as the first touch of water on a cold day. Betty was a shadow undressing, undressed, approaching the bed. A black bare-breasted shadow placing itself beside me on the white sheets, saying, 'Come on, take off your clothes.' And the brass bedstead gleam covered by a red dress carelessly hung. To be thrown away tomorrow when the new one came. Tomorrow Monday. The first day of school, and hardly a day to be buying dresses. Would I have to tell her that? 'You the slowest undresser I ever saw.' 'It's getting cold.' 'Well, hurry up and take off those wet things.' 'Blow out the lamp.' 'I like it up. I want to see you.' 'How about people looking in from outside?' But there were already others who never should have been allowed looking on, and from within the room itself, Betty did not need to laugh, mimicking, '. . . people looking in from outside . . .' Already there was the baleful, vacant stare of Anthony, an accusing grimace from Hille, and the child. What kind of a look from the child, certain to be uneasy in Betty's womb? 'Take off your clothes.' Hille always took off her things in the dark, and never had she seen me naked in the light. But Anthony, was he watching me, or Betty? Neither one of us, really. He looked on like a man who had no choice but to be there, taking in the room, while hung up on a deeper pull to be elswhere. 'Take off your clothes.' I took off my damp shirt and went to the basin to slosh water on my bloodied hand and face.

The cold water raised goose pimples on my neck and arms, and I wanted to see exactly what kind of scar Anthony had put on my face. But the mirror was over the other side of the room, on the other side of Betty and the bed. She was restless. She made the springs squeak impatiently. Anthony and Hille waited to see what I would do. Betty waited for what she hoped I would do. And I took as much time as I could drying with a towel that smelled faintly of some other man's body. I could hear the music coming again from the schoolhouse. I could hear other sounds in the night too — owls, a dog, someone snoring in the other half of Betty's house. But nowhere could I hear the sound of a bus, and that would have been the nicest sound of all. 'You going to stand there all night getting off that blood?' Betty asked. 'Stop frowning so,' she said. 'You don't have anything to worry about.' Then, still managing not to see her directly, doing what I could to protect my naked self from the light, I took off the rest of my clothes and got into bed beside her. Hille's grimace became more acute, Anthony's expression did not change. Betty was hot. Her touch was far hotter than mine, and more certain. Come have your fun. Her hands groped about my body, and her flaring nostrils blew strong and close beneath my face. Her eyes teased and assured at the same time, but I could have told her it was no use. 'You're goin' to buy me a little red dress?' she said, and kissed my neck. I closed my eyes, and behind their darkness tried to revive her as the mysterious dream-plaguing creature finally captured and about to be unmasked, but it had all happened already. The coldness that had started at my neck and face encroached steadily downwards though I was trying to hold it. 'Turn off the light,' I said. 'Uhh uhh. I like it like this.' The mystery had already flown to some new hiding place. Flown completely. Disappeared. Nothing but the smooth sheets, and Betty lying there equally smooth, but soft and hot where I was cold. The coldness rolled down and I could not stop it. I lay paralysed. 'What's the matter?' Betty asked as I lolled lifelessly in her hand.

She blew her hot breath against my skin, but it was useless. I did not stir. I tried giving her Hille's face, (No. That had never happened before — well, not quite that way. There was the first time with Hille, but that time I got sick) (No. I wasn't tired, and I wasn't afraid. It was just the coldness) tried bringing back the smell of her sister's old servant room, but none of that worked. Betty at last reached up and turned off the light. Too late. 'You tired?' she asked. 'Tired,' I mumbled. 'Next time come see me before you fight with Anthony. He just a boy too, but he can kill.' She said that, but Anthony made no kill that night, for after Betty turned down the lamp both he and Hille disappeared. Perhaps if this had not come too late, and if the sounds of the dance band was not half lost on the breeze, Betty might have earned her new red dress, and I a restful night beside her. 'Do you want me to make some Ovaltine?' she asked. 'No.' 'It will help you go to sleep. You should sleep a little bit, then when I wake you up you'll feel better.' 'I don't want to sleep.' Betty sighed. She stretched out on her stomach, and I could sense the disappointment overtaking her.

I did not buy Betty a red dress, nor a blue one, nor any kind of dress. While I lay sleepless, crushed with guilt and grieving, she managed to subdue whatever frustration she might have felt in sleep. She did not hear the five o'clock bus moaning past the pond, coming to the cricket ground. Neither did she stir while I slipped out of bed, drew on my clothes hurriedly, and gathered up my bundle. And if she did awake, if she called, I did not hear, as I dashed from her house out into the brisk morning, making it to the road just in time to stand full in the oncoming headlights and wave the driver down. He was coming on fast too, gave me no time to disguise myself from the late dancers, fresh from the hall, who had stepped onto the grassy bank along the road to let him pass. They saw. And even as the rattling old bus coughed and shimmied away with me just barely on the running-board, I heard the laughter go up, and I was

thankful that I had managed against losing my hat, or anything
from the bundle that would have had to be left behind.

Saturday morning. 12th

Hille kept saying she was my woman. (I'm yours, baby. You're
my man.)

I was never anybody's man. How the hell could I be anybody's man?

In one moment, 'Talk to me! Don't you dare look at me like
that.' In another, 'You don't need to say a thing, baby. I'm
your woman.'

Hille is not Cleo. There is no mystery about her, and her
armpits smell of perfumed deodorant.

Hille never could be Cleo. Her teeth make no half-moon
in the dark, there is no cunning in her eyes. She tried very
hard at keeping us joined though, and sometimes I came close
to loving her for that. I came close to loving her too when she
said, 'No need to talk, baby' because then she cracked me so I
could spill words, phrases, intentions, dreams until I felt
purged. I am the mute generation, became so because 'speech
is silver, silence is gold.' Silence is all that's real. No words,
no lies. And yet I have never lost the urge to speak. An urge
which never ceased growling within like a ravenous cannibal.
Chew me up if it wasn't released. Bite of a mad dog; a touch of
madness. What a horror! impending madness. Even so, no
words. I repeat, NO WORDS NO WORDS in search of others who
understand and speak no-words. I admire liars. It is a pity I
have such trouble being one. I understand something that
should put me among the best liars of all — lies also tell the
truth. But I am afraid. Above all, I am quite afraid not only of
telling the truth, but of simply telling. There, that's the truth!
I am afraid of telling because it is ugly and I have yet to meet
someone who respects ugliness. Everybody's got it, but that's
a well-guarded secret. '. . . who knows but that, on the lower

158

frequencies, I speak for you ... ? Yeah! Who knows? Everybody knows. But that's all right. [That's one of my favourite sayings, especially when Nothing ain't right.] I'll endure. Rivers, valleys, heaven and hell, not one of them older than me. I'll endure ...

Hille never stood still long enough for me to get hold of her. 'I can't understand why you would ever want to leave here,' she said. 'Don't you love Trinidad?'

And it was useless answering, what does loving Trinidad have to do with anything, or the price of tea, as was one time the fashion. She kept right on. 'I don't see how anybody could ever want to get away from a place this beautiful.' Meaning, of course, my village which she had never seen, only heard about from me myself who ever tried to tell how grotesque life was there, how painful and molesting against virtue, honour, and all the other grand things I learned about from the Reverend's books.

Yet, those were the days when I thought I was happy. Hille and I were together constantly, and my skin was getting accustomed to the stares, my ears developing enough wit to anticipate the dirty calls. And they came, the stares, the slang, hostile or malicious, whenever Hille and I were together but not alone. On the orphanage grounds it was the boys who made most noise. 'Ah, ah! Look at teacher Marcus! Miss Hille, you gon' marry him?' Or sometimes one rushed up and defiantly thrusting himself between us seized her hand and stared at me. Hille loved the boys' innocent faces. I don't know what she did for the Director, but after that first reprimand he had no further words for me on the subject of Miss Hille and myself.

Hille insisted on taking my hand whenever we walked down to the wharves. We went down Frederick Street window shopping, or sat in Marine Square in the shade of a plane tree, always close together.

In those days I had her scent in my nostrils constantly, fore of the burnt-tar and fish smell of the wharves, the heavy sweet fumes of flowers in the Botanical Gardens, the odoration of clogged sewers and sweating bodies on hot days. And in touching, our pulses joined their own rhythm which set up barriers against the noises of the City. So that it was from afar off that I heard the rattling tram cars, the market's squabble, stevedores swearing, an occasional aeroplane.

In the dome of this silence rhythmed by our joined pulses, we walked down George Street to the crowded roti shop, where they pressed against us. The cinema crowd of a late Friday night, with the hard, fierce men looking past our shoulders, missing our faces with their eyes, but pressing against us. With eyes quick, defiant, inside juts of glistening cheeks, they looked like monstrous rodents. And the women, not quite as hard as their men but equally fierce, pressing against us too, only not with their torsos but with elbows and knees, whatever bony projection they could use to let us know they could make life uncomfortable. Ramjohn behind the counter was slow, and we waited amidst the waspish fumes of burning oil and flour, peppered curry stew; hemmed in by the prickly smell of sweat pressing against us on three sides, and the voices going by, over, around, but never aimed at us, going by steadily. 'Ramjohn, I don't want no chinkiness on the meat!' 'Man you see what Tarzan do with them Zulus?' 'Them wasn't Zulus, you fool. Zulus in South Africa and Tarzan ain't never set foot there.' 'Well I don't care what they was — man you see how their eyes open big when Tarzan fly down out of the tree?' 'The first one he hit went down like a dead dog!' 'With one hand . . .! He take the chief with one hand!' 'That black African stand up there rolling his eyes, and let Tarzan do like he want with him — I wish it was me.' 'You a African?' 'You can beat Tarzan, eh?' 'I ain't saying all that. But I ain't no damn fool to stand up and let . . .' 'We know, we know. You're a real bad man. You worse than Jesse James. You'd a show just how clean your heels is!' Everybody laughs. 'You're all a bunch of stupid fools. That's just a picture — ain't nobody beating or killing nobody. That's just fake. Johnny Weissmuller and them darky boys the best of friends in Hollywood.' 'You hear him? "darky boys" just like he's a Yankee himself.' 'Best of friends hell! You read what they do to black people in the States? How they hang them up in trees and cut their balls out!' 'That's not the States, that's Africa!' 'Same difference . . .' 'But you're a bunch of stupid fools! You standing up here quarrelling about Tarzan and all them fake black people, and the coolie man here picking out your eyes. Ramjohn! put some more meat in that roti. My woman ain't no whore.' High class and low class, they were the ones on George Street — aside from the merchants — with shillings to spare. Whores.

Hille forked our fingers fiercely, and in an instant I felt the sweat come between our palms. She held hard, and though we had been there several times before, fright, or terror, or whatever still made the corner of her mouth twitch, while she tried to fix her face so it seemed she was smiling. The sweat came steadily while they followed us down the three midnight blocks, still talking about Tarzan and his heroics, except when a woman's voice said, 'But she skinny, eh! I can't see what he find in her.' 'Like a damn skeleton,' a man's voice joined. 'You ain't mean that,' the woman's voice came back. 'If you had a chance you'd be chasing her white ass just like a damn dog.' 'Ah, gwan.' Voices following until we came to the funeral home, and climbed away beside it to my room.

'Is that true?' Hille asked.

'What?'

'What the woman said.'

'What?'

'About him wanting to chase my white ass like a dog.'

'I don't know.'

'How come you don't know? Isn't that the way you feel?'

'You calling me a dog?'

'Stop being funny.'

'Never seen the colour of your ass.'

'All right. Be funny if you have to. But, seriously, would it have been different between us if I wasn't white?'

'Different how?'

She stomped the floor. 'Stop being a fool and answer me.' Screaming 'Would it have been, could it have been any different between us were I not a white woman?' Maybe not screaming, but enunciating clearly in a loud voice.

I laughed. That was the easiest way to deal with her tempers, and her talk about being serious. 'Too late now,' I said.

'You make me sick,' she said. 'Do you hear? You make me sick. You and your sensitivities! "I have to go back to Africa",' (mimicking now), '" I have to collect the pieces of myself scattered in Spain, and Brussels, and Liverpool, and Marseille" — and you can't take a simple trip to the Mainland. You'll never take a trip anywhere! I ask you a simple question — Could you have loved me if I were black like you, and you can't answer.' (Screaming for certain now.) 'What do you want with me? What do you want with me?' Screaming and dashing for the door. But I barred the way and she fell back into the chair crying. Her hands folding the dress down into her lap, bony knees bare. She sobbed with a terrible shaking, and I didn't know what to do about it.

The rains started later, and fell all night. We did not go back to the orphan home.

Hille said, 'I didn't mean to cry. I didn't mean all that I said about you either. We'll go to France together. And Spain too — and Africa. I don't really want to see dirty old England. Let's put that off till last. I mean, real last.'

We laughed.

We had to keep the windows latched, and we made quite a lot of sweat. We drank tea.

Hille's hair drooped flat, her face became coarse and smudgy. The sheets were damp, and so were the curtains and our clothes. Hille moved the room around. She moved the bed from beneath the window and put the table there. She shifted the morris chair so one could read in it by the lamp on the table, and she covered the dingy cushions with a clean sheet.

After the rain stopped we looked outside, but there was no sun. It was a dingy Saturday. All the wooden verandahs along George Street were soaked black, and the sky was still heavy. The city seemed silent, as though waiting to make sure of the sky's intentions before cranking itself into action again.

Hille and I put on our damp clothes and walked down St Vincent Street to the post office where she picked up her letters. Then we turned uptown, towards the Savannah, where the goalposts, the grandstands stood soaked and grey, same as all the wooden store fronts and verandahs we had passed on our way down. We walked across the wet grass. Once on the other side we were so near the Gardens we could not resist, and soon we passed through the slanting wire gate, into the dimness and silence of the first dripping trees. They were all spattered and dull. The palms and bamboo, the giant ferns, begonias, the countless bushes with names I can't remember — they were all dull and drooping.

'Darling,' Hille said, 'I feel weak.' I caught her around the waist. 'Do you love me?' she said; and I don't know what I said but it was not no, certainly must have been something to imply yes while being really in the nature of maybe. It is strange I do not remember what I answered. I usually remember such things well. 'Do you love me?' and then, 'I'm so filled with love I feel weak. Let's sit down.' We found a bench that was green where its paint had not peeled, and Hille leaned herself against me. Her pulse was fast where I felt it at her wrist and neck, then mine raced too. We sat for a long time. She read her letters. One was from her father in Chicago, the other from Harry in Virginia. The first sent money, the second a photograph with love. Hille tucked them both in her raincoat pocket. 'Would it be wrong to stay with you forever?' she asked. 'Why wrong?' and I should have added, I want you to stay forever, forever, more than anything in the world; but I didn't. Heart clamoured, but lips refused. 'Why wrong?' 'I don't know,' she said. 'It might make trouble for both of us.'

'But not wrong,' I said.

'Do you want me to stay?'

'Yes, I do. Do you want to stay?'

'I do.'

Then we sat quietly again for a long time.

At last I knew there would be no rambling back and forth across the sea. There would be no need. Marseille and Brussels, Madrid and Liverpool, Amsterdam, they had come to me, or, rather, they had sent me an offering. I looked at her — this female cupped out of the loins of the masters, herself destined to be a mother of masters, she was much and little at the same time. And the thing that was much about her was untouchable.

It was from there under the trees that I led us to my village. 'Let's go,' I said. 'Let's go somewhere.' 'Where?' Hille asked, with a little smile that opened her teeth and curled the corners of her lips. 'Let's go to the village,' I said. 'Oh!' she said, and clapped her hands. We were on our way.

On the bus Hille was thrilled to be riding in the midst of all the returning market wives with their broad aprons, and head-ties, and baskets still half full of chickens, greens, and ground provisions that had not sold that day. They glanced at us — some smiled, many frowned, but none said hello.

At the head of the village we got off the bus, and the bus-stop idlers were there, under the cedar trees. There had been no rain in the village. We walked past, and although I knew them all, only one or two said hello when I raised a hand in greeting. The others just stared, or looked away pretending not to see. Yet we had not gone far before I became aware three or four were loosely following us. When we came to the heart of the village where the houses between large plum and mango trees crowded the road on both sides and shut out the canefields behind, our followers had increased to a little bunch, I could tell from the slap of their feet and the voices.

We did not stop at Grandfather's house. I said, 'Grandfather lives there,' and we passed on hand in hand — Hille's pulse still bounding sharply, but mine now a beat or two behind.

Five o'clock, the hour before dusk, the hour between work and play which is the most playful hour of all in the village. New woodsmoke from some kitchens, and the sun still hot, but the shadows stretched out like early ghosts in the sinking light. And at the centre of the village lounged the evening idlers, many of whom had cheered me time after time in younger days when I raced with Anthony. I raised a hand and was answered in a low murmur, but I could tell, they were mostly seeing Hille. And after we passed along I could hear the voices, the talking in words not clear enough for me to understand, but coming behind, following at a distance not too close, and the superficially aimless slow feet dragging through the dust. The same kind of hard men who pressed us so at Ramjohn's — except these were less like rodents. No fierce and eager glitter to their eyes, they looked at Hille remote from some far place behind dull peeps, flat barriers between them and the world. And I chuckled to myself and pressed her arm, until she pulled away, saying, 'Aren't they marvellous?' Meaning the dried-down men with trousers rolled up, their toes grabbing dust with each step. 'Why don't you ever walk like that? The city spoiled you.'

Hille had never seen canefields before, and she thought they were beautiful. She had never had a blazing sun in February before, and she thought that was beautiful. Nor had she ever seen the hard men with all ten toes splayed and thickly cal-loused from too many days against the hot earth. She thought they were beautiful too. And the women — not so dried as the men, some even audaciously fat, bloated. Draw-string skirts hugged tight beneath their breasts falling away over fertile and tragic wombs like voluminous mysteries, brushing left-right

165

the tops of the toes also splayed and mightily calloused. 'How beautiful they are!' she said. 'How magnificent! What carriage! Do you see the way they hold their heads? Nobody ever walks like that in the mid-west.' Nobody in the mid-west ever carried caneloads the only way it was possible for a woman to carry caneloads — bundled on the head. Nobody in the mid-west perhaps ever carried such loads beneath which to hold the neck steady was a question of eat or starve. But I was too slow and only thought of that much later. 'I'd love to have seen your mother walk. Wasn't she beautiful?' And as one must when faced with such a question about one's mother, I replied, 'She was. Everybody said so.' The truth is, I don't remember my mother well enough to tell whether she was beautiful or not. She moved softly, that I remember. But apart from a low-browed dusky face with eyes that mostly looked on, and a mouth that seldom smiled yet was never sorrowful, I don't remember much about how my mother looked. I remember her voice — singing bits of hymns and the latest calypsos indiscriminately.

'Everybody here is beautiful,' Hille said. 'They're so free — so free! I never went barefoot in all my life. Not even as a child,' she added, taking off her shoes.

We walked down the hot gravel road — the same I had walked so many times as a child, and there was nothing new about it. Down the slope behind us were the village houses, ahead of us the factory, with its single chimney towering from the folds of soot-stained buildings like a giant erect grey penis. And the road itself unchanged between the giant sentinel palms tall and whispery on both sides, their trunks covered with dust and soot raised by the mule teams and locomotives. Crop-time it was, but still the season of fitful rains, so that in a minute the sun disappeared, the rain came pelting down in big drops. There was no shelter except the conspiring trees, and once we were standing with our backs fast against the smooth palm trunk Hille whooped and cried, 'Magnificent! Beautiful! What a

166

place!' A long trickle came down the trunk and spread out around her shoulders. It went down her back, and she wiggled, giggling. Then in a flash she dropped her shoes, dashed out from beneath the branches, and all the villagers who had followed us and were themselves plastered against their own trees craned their necks to see — this beautiful shiny-haired American lady, who had left her shoes behind and was out prancing in the rain. Just to watch her jump up and around with the hair plastered around her skull, and her thin shapeless cotton dress soaked to her skin, showing the outline of her pants and bra. They came out laughing, and she laughed too — blew them kisses and came back running to get her shoes, saying 'Aren't they marvellous? So free!' And by then they felt free to follow her coming back and pick me up too with their eyes and voices. 'Pappa Jay's boy!' Milling around the wet tree. 'Boy I thought you never was goin' turn round and give me the time of day!' 'Ain't nothing unmannerly about that boy.' 'I know that. But he never turned round . . .' It was true. I had purposely not turned around from the moment the bus dropped us at the head of the village. Purposely! Always discovering purpose later on, and so saying purposely, as if I knew from the beginning what purpose led me to bring Hille back to the village in the first place. But it is not so. From the moment they picked me up, 'Pappa Jay's boy,' with their eyes on Hille . . . No! Not so. In the moment I let them pick us up, sweep us along the muddy road with the rising smell of beaten weeds and scattered palm blossoms and mud too through which Hille barefoot squelched pulps between her toes, in that moment with the roadside ravine trickling a roaring hiss off into the fields, and black birds chirping and a cleansed breeze shaking light drops from the clustered fronds, in that moment with the sun just starting to come back again, a crescented sliver on the horizon, the near fields, all else standing grey and still, in that moment when I felt far too weary to hold them off, to say No, we will not go with you this day to the rumshop or any other place you have in mind, I felt not only weariness but a wide joy too, and must have known without knowing that some duty was about to get done, that I was about to make my delivery and claim rest at last. And at the rumshop, that awkward octagonal hut perched on crazy stilt pillars with its overhang gallery crumbling in places, the floor worn smooth to the heels of countless buyers who ever paid in sweat and body grease, here I must have known again without knowing that I was simply waiting for the end, the coup de grâce which it was my duty to deliver, and which would inevitably occur. Those who hang out in rumshops or around them are always waiting — for a new action, for release from a long ago action. Grin and wait.

They danced. The thick-soled men shuffled about Hille. Sometimes hiding her altogether with quick thrusting slants of their bodies, waving and weaving like sensuous cobras, then the step away, fluid as light with no break in the rhythm of slurring bellies. I watched. Heard Hille panting, 'I can't understand why you ever would want to leave here. Don't you just love these people?' Not knowing herself that that was all passed — the wanting to leave. Not knowing that with each step down the palm-lined road I had understood better how weary I had become. Understood in a feeling way, so that first the muscles knew, then whatever is in between, and finally the bones began. But the mind, itself unfeeling, remained unhearing, proud at having borne me for so long, irreversible in its commitment to see me through. The mind, it kept me from sliding into a ditch beside the road and stretching out in the warm mud; it put off dealing with that invitation coming through my nostrils — the smell of earth inviting its own to come back; put it off upon the shadows, upon shadows that had really grown much too long and could do nothing else but disappear. And with the darkness, peace, until the return of morning. It might have helped if I knew how to put off being weary — if I could simply have managed to resist and fend it off. Yet, all I could remember doing is laughing like a damned fool. Not laughing either, come to think of it — except on the inside — but grinning on and on, even after my cheeks ached and the muscles of my lips went stiff: on and on, furiously never letting myself roar once, nor scream once. They picked at and poked her as they would have a strange poulet in the market. Not the women. They hung back, or said to me I was looking good; or interrogating with a tinge of hostility, 'When you goin' get married boy?' A steadier grin, another drink — for me who never touched a bottle since leaving Pappa Jay's but suddenly now like some sort of hero come home accepting drink after drink; with Hille half-way down the counter crying, 'Marvellous! Just marvellous! You people drive me out of my mind! You're beautiful!' And one more stubble face lashes out with black knotty hands, snatching Hille's and all the other knotty hands drumming down the counter, picking up force again, others joining in upon the casks piled one on top of the other over against the wall. Grin, who from the beginning knew it could only come to that.

The improvised drumming interfered with my pulse, but I did no more than tap a foot, or drum lightly with my hand against the counter. CLATTER-RAM, CLATTER-RAM, CLATTER-RUR-RAM! through the length of the rumshop, with Hille prancing up and down on her toes, not graceful, not really awkward either, simply lost. Prancing up and down, the damp hair still fast to her head, her face shining high red, her eyes turned out so I knew there was hardly any sight left looking at herself from inside. One old man took her first by the hands to show her how to jerk the belly. He swivelled, then let loose. A magnificent flurry of stabbings from the waist. Everybody howled — laughter and cheering. He was a challenge, and Hille, passed from hand to hand, tried her best too to make that successive offering of ass and belly in rhythm, but not quite getting it because the separation of back and behind did not work too well for her. Then one with his arms around her waist squared off, his knees jammed to hers, showing her how. 'This way. Like this, girl, This how you do it,' with his bony ass flying. And she squared off too, only she couldn't hump the air without looking like a mechanical doll, and everyone laughed. Everyone except the descendant of Amerigo de Vespucci behind the counter. He, son in the fourteenth generation of that venerable sailor who gave his name to the New World, he did not laugh. His lips remained puckered out, his jaw hostile, and were he not committed to a heritage of merchandising — rum in this case — he would most certainly have been going after his share of blood. Overlord and slave concurrent to his black patrons, he popped the bottles for those drinking stout, drew glasses of puncheon for the others, with never a smile cracking his face, wiping his fingers on the smudged apron cloth around his lard middle, Amerigo's line is no longer trim. Pushing back the hair — mostly bunched grease-curled ringlets — from his florid brow. He kept his black hawk's eye steadfastly averted from where the white girl danced, kept them averted and to himself, except to look staggering Samuel up and down once with a vituperous 'Scum! Feelthy neegar scum!' but passing Samuel the rum anyway. Until old Hines up and jumped her.

Old Hines, greybeard deacon of our Baptist church, who had humped the best in our village, and several other villages, suddenly let out a cry and jumped her. From behind. Hille flung a bewildered look over her shoulder, with suddenly her eyes come home. And everyone laughed. Except Amerigo XV. He dropped a glass, wiped his fingers, pushed back his curls, and huffed like a red frog close to exploding. Hille didn't know what to do. One had her by the waist in front, and Hines had her around the belly from behind, working her close like a dog. She looked to me, for me, but when our eyes met I smiled and clapped the rhythm. 'Get her out of here!' Amerigo screamed. 'Goddamn! You! You!' pushing on my shoulder, 'Get her out of here. I don't care if she is the daughter of Harry Truman! Get her out of here.' At that instant catching, unbelieving and knowing at the same time it had to be so, Anthony's face racing through the door. My blood, scenting enemy, moved a

170

split second faster than the mind, and even before recognizing what I was about to do I had intercepted Anthony, and the collision took us both to the floor. He struggled at first, but the motive blood burning at top speed under the bare surface of my skin knew his struggles could make no difference. And in short time, his throat between my thumbs and fingers, he lay still except for the eyes bulging from their sockets, the tongue slowly coming out of his throat. The grandfathers and Amerigo succeeded in heaving me off him then, but they could neither keep me away nor protect him from the blood cry in which I was consumed. They could not protect him from the pickle cask which my demon raised high — I could never lift one before or afterwards — and brought smashing down on his skull. Some said I never lifted the cask at all, that it came crashing down by accident. I remember feeling extremely weak and frightened after the crash died, and Anthony lay with his smashed face poked up between two broken staves, his blood running thin in the pickle juice splashed all around the floor.

Monday, July 14, 1952

How does it seem when you recall the face of one you killed, look into his eyes, see his cheeks, his nose, his mouth, his forehead, look into all this and see your own? Above all the eyes, your eyes, that refuse any longer to hide? How does it seem? Yesterday I knew.

Last night I thought I knew and understood many things, and I went to bed with a satisfied mind. The mirror said around its crack — a scar S from left top to right bottom — fine. Everything was fine. Fly specks, soap specks — black pimples in the lamplight — disappearing where covered by the cheek and forehead and chin, but not where the teeth gleamed yes, everything is fine. Fly specks, soap specks, food specks too, from spitting at the mirror while cleaning the teeth. What fine teeth! Broad, even, white. Whatever happened to Grandfather's slave photos with the hands, neck, and feet, but not all the face black? White eyes, white teeth — reflections. Only white in black could look so scared, so sad. Eyes and teeth dominant, trapped between folds and folds of black, dominant, defiant jelly fear; white vulnerability of an egg, and ivory bravura. Even in the old slave's face in Grandfather's photograph — a face all whorls and slants, flying bulbous cheeks, a disappearing brow and nose disappeared except for two forward intake funnels, round lips. I am black as he was black. I have his teeth, his eyes. But where he was round and soft, I am lean and full of sharp edges. What a self to admire! Satisfied before the mirror, even as I saw it all again like an implacable procession of animated photographs — Anthony coming in through the doorway, one knee raised, slanting and lean himself, expressionless face except for the moment when his eyes picked up Hille. And next her face, contracting from that broad jelly terror to a swift and concentrated glow of reprieve. Sister and brother; born of the same womb, or perhaps out of each other. Predicament, and commitment, twin halves of a single moment; only there was a third half to the moment on review, called itself destiny. Designed precisely to prevent the moment from being born, to hold those two identical complements apart, forever deny any peace, any of that vulnerable, corruptible, but inescapably unique oneness glimmering through the vision of reprieve. No peace. I am Shango son of Yemaya, angel of devastation and silence!

Yes, my destiny was clear. Last night as it passed again through my mind I saw, and I knew that the conjunctive moment had long ago been fated. Long before Anthony, Hille or I had been realized in seed it had been determined precisely how our lives should flourish or bend in the moment of that meeting. So I went to sleep satisfied. Would have awakened satisfied too, had the Inspector — God damn his soul — left my dreams alone. He came soft footing in, grinning like a lackey, offering me my mother. 'Here t'is sir. £10.3, and very well bought, sir.' Offering me the mother who should have seen father on into his rejoicing. But father never rejoiced. I the great American fringe citizen will see no rejoicing. I am too sore. Even as the Inspector held out the package, offering, I ached all through to the bone and couldn't raise my arms. '£10.3 sir. An enjoyable package if ever there were one.' Aching, frozen, neither would my arms move nor my voice speak. The Inspector chuckling, 'Do you think the price unfair? Tell you then, sir, you've been a good boy. Quite a good boy really, and I'll let you have this one for nothing.' Frozen in every bone. Arms, legs, fingers, and feet. A long fight. And that's really what the dream was. I had been in a long fight, three hundred rounds and more in a ring that had the sun for its only spotlight, a fight during which I played straight man while he hit me every blow he could find. The overhead light was hot, and after all my sweat was gone, body grease came, a little at a time, the way grease comes. Weary through and through, but he didn't seem the least bit tired. It was I who ached arm-weary, wanting just to lie down, but too weary for that even, because it meant fighting off the whatever it was that kept me going on. He did all the work. All I did was stand straight and be hurt, yet he never looked as tired as I felt, and, of course, he wasn't bleeding the way I was either. The red marks on his body were mostly from my blood spattering. And in my ear I could hear nothing but a struggle to breathe, in my sight, what little I had left, see nothing but a white blur dancing. That is exterior sight. Internally it was all red, explosion after explosion, all red. And just when I was finally ready to let myself go and butt him once he disappeared, to come back in a flash all dressed, his body washed and clean, his hair every strand in place, his eyes elevated, showing less memory of the fight he had just halted than a strange wariness. 'You been a good boy' he said. 'Take this,' offering the same thing I couldn't at first believe was my mother, dressed in a calico print smock — bright red flowers but long the way village women wear their skirts long to hide themselves from everything but the imagination. 'Free, deserved

173

or not. I'll let you have it free . . . ' as finally I managed to get my reflexes together and push away, ease out. But when I got all the way out of the dream I was still sweating, and my mouth still tasted like warm blood.

And I lay thinking about The Undertaker downstairs, not because I felt he was a good thing to be thinking about, but because just at that moment I heard them getting ready to go off after a body, and from far away now near, understood that I had heard them make the same noises hundreds of times, so that I could forecast. And when I found myself feeling just a little ahead of what they would have to do next I lay thinking about the man downstairs, keeping very still. I would give him nothing to go on. Or maybe he had gotten so he could read my quietness, so I would have to remember to make strange noises to keep him off track. His attendants swearing at whoever dared to die at that hour of the morning, equipment going into the hearse with a rough clatter, and I could recognize horses, cooling chest, sack of ice, setting the firm tempo around which lighter things fluttered. Then the door slam. Churning engine, finally exploding into a feathery roar. The driver would have all the dead know he was coming. He was about to take the road. Beware! while the engine cried and screamed like a tormented animal ready to pounce on anything in its path. They were off. I lay thinking about the man downstairs, and the Inspector, the one-two punch that tampered with my night sufficiently so there could be no getting back to sleep, until daylight came in around the window edges, came in behind the early milk-cart trundling its way down George Street. And before getting up I knew to myself that today was going to be a long day.

Last night I went to sleep satisfied, but this morning, 'Black man, you're a loser, you're a loser Black man, and where, when, what, make no difference — they will ever be the same. How? That's the only question. And if you had a son that's what would have made the difference — how? Your style. Your style, Black man — that's how to save a son, if you had a son, if you had a

174

son — STYLE! beyond you not to lose, you're a born loser. And when the time comes, in whatever place it comes, then the best foot forward — lay it down in style that counts for a son. And who knows? maybe he will end up winning. Winning? Maybe. It could be — if there were a son, if there were a son, if there were a son — END! but you know you can't stop when you know, you know you can't stop when you know, you know you can't ... ' that's this morning.

What do you know Black man?

It is somewhere hidden. Somewhere beneath the jumble of faces and smells and bitter tastes.

That's all in your imagination, Black man — smells, and faces, and bitter tastes. All in your imagination. Dreaming. There is balance in the real world — sweet to be found wherever bitter rears. There's sweet in the world Black man! have you ever thought of that? Get up off your lazy ass and find the sweetness in the world. It is there. It will tame the bitterness in your imagination.

Today is going to be a long day — but not half long enough. At this moment I am no nearer telling what it is I know and have to tell than I was before I learned to speak. I must have known back then too, back then before the tutor and his books, before Hille and her 'You're a free man', known it all, just like I know it all now. But telling! Seems I need more than a single lifetime in which to get that done properly. Even after all the talking with myself. Today is going to be a long day, but not long enough.

It was with that in mind that I left my room this morning and strolled into the thick of the city.

July begins the hottest season of the year, and at seven this morning wisps of a late dawn breeze lingered still, but whatever freshness it had brought down the hills before sunrise had been all burned away. I strolled out thinking for a moment I would walk to the orphan home and see my boys, but that didn't last long. It was dumb to think of them as my boys anyway. They are

175

nobody's boys, they are ownerless. And I always treated them as such. I set out instead for the Square, taking my time, savouring the shadows, and calmly taking the sun on the back of my neck where it pierced through between the buildings. George Street is a narrow street, a rotting street. It smelled like a disinfected wound going raw, but nobody seemed to care.

The government clerks strolling in twos and threes or coasting down on their bicycles to the Red House already had the collars of their starched shirts damp. The salesgirls tripped under broken platoons of pretty parasols. The street vendors' brows were beaded, even those crouched under the shade of their mobile overhangs. I stopped once for a coconut, and the Indian, blacker than Mahatma Gandhi, took four nonchalant strokes with his cutlass — three for the heavy damp fibre around the nut, one cracking the nut itself, skimming, but not breaking the jelly — then screwed out the jelly and handed me the drink. It was very sweet, very cool. 'Good coconut, eh!' he said. I nodded my head. 'Have another one?' 'No,' I said. 'Have another one,' he said. 'This big one here's the same price — twelve cents,' he said, spearing one on the tip of his cutlass. I looked at the yellowing bulge of husk over the nut's eyes and smiled at him. He smiled too and dropped the nut back into the cart. 'Twelve cents,' he said. I paid. Reaching somewhere in a ragged pocket for change he said, 'I'll let you have that big one for eight cents,' I shook my head. He handed back my change, and returned to squatting in the shade of his cart.

A clock somewhere struck the quarter hour, and the shuffle of bodies along the sidewalk became more intense. Suddenly the street was overcrowded — cars, bicycles, carts, and buses. And in this last quarter hour before eight o'clock I found myself propped against the northern gate into the Square, facing our 'national character'. Indeed. We are not a nation, but that has nothing to do with our having or not having a national character. So I stood with my shoulder against the rusty iron gate — relic of an age when Spanish dons dipped knees before their women

— stood there with the sun searching through my shirt and skin to where it made the sweat glands prickle, facing our national character. It hurried by. It had many colours — brown, light-brown, dark-brown, in-between-brown, yellow-brown, black-brown, black, yellow, red, once-in-a-while-white. Come to think of it, that's not too many colours, but that's what I saw. Our national character had different shapes — round, lean, flat, bulky, zig-zagged; and heights — tall, short, all levels of in-between. Different colours, different hair, different voices, this national character smiled, it chatted, sulked, scowled, it cursed and laughed and looked cheerful. It said 'good morning' or didn't see, begged my pardon or trundled over my feet belligerently. And I stood there until the clock struck eight strokes against the hearts of all late employees before I realized I felt nothing. I did not feel a thing. I stood there and watched the final crusade of hurrying legs, the buses, the bikes, the motor-cars, and didn't feel a thing. Finally had to stop kidding myself and admit I didn't give a damn about anybody's national character. I was standing there, hoping someone would find me. And someone almost did, only I didn't want to see her. So just as the terrible clock, wherever it was, lay down its last quivering stroke, I ducked away.

That was on my mind too before I left my room, especially as I went past The Undertaker's window, because it was something we had once joked about. 'Suppose I died this minute, what would you do?' 'Send for the man downstairs,' Hille had answered. 'Is there something else I should do?' The man downstairs, I glimpsed him this morning as I came down the steps, sitting, as always, framed between his window and the display coffins and caskets in his shop, sipping tea. He looks a very tall man sitting down, but one day I caught him standing and saw that he was without legs and tall from the waist up only. But straight in the back, very stiff and straight in the back all the way to the crown of his head. Mongoloid eyes, caucasoid lips, an African nose and brow, he wears them all; and his complexion belongs to everybody. The man downstairs. And she had said, 'Send for the man downstairs! Is there something else I should do?' while knowing all the time I averted my eyes when we passed his window. Hille never missed much. She must have noticed that I always managed never to look at him sitting there surrounded by his glistening boxes, waiting. Never look at him fully, anyway. She always said, 'You're too superstitious.' And she never answered my question, 'Suppose I died this minute, what would you do?' She kept hearing it as '. . . what would you do with me?' and that wasn't what I meant at all. It would have satisfied, I suppose, to hear her say, 'Weep forever,' or 'Kill myself,' although not really, not so much as to hear her say, 'Don't know.' That was what I would have liked to hear and she never said it. We knew why, both of us. We understood that should I die, there would be no chaos left behind, there would in fact be great peace. Her womb would then be released from contracting minus sperm and she could return to birthing baby colossi.

So I dodged away from Hille.

I dodged away, but just far enough into the crowd so I could see her without her seeing me, and I watched her go by. She walked like a bird — mincing, pigeon-toed steps, her shanks angled forward, slight points at the knee and rear, a straight back. I watched her go by, watched the sun glistening on her hair coiffed atop her head like a silken, delicate crown, and in her red face the two eyes perked, intent, fixed on whatever it was she was going towards. I followed, to see where she was going. At a safe distance. From a safe distance my eyes played up and down the spine of my sparrow, and despite all that's happened, for a moment or two I had little leapings of joy on the inside. Flesh never forgets flesh. I followed the way she threw her skinny arm back and forth as she minced, followed the rise and fall of her almost absent behind, and couldn't stop trembling at the quick erotic memories that came, bringing close with them the smell of her naked and sweating. 'How could you?' I said aloud

178

to myself. 'How could you?' Especially when the time I had seen her last was that clattering moment before Anthony went down, and then only out of the corner of an eye because I was intent on him, a swift glimpse out of the corner of one eye that caught horror on her face, for she was about to go down too — only I didn't know that at the time — and in that moment there was nary an erotic twitch, nothing but the deep feeling of a bond broken somewhere, a flood released, and the magic headiness of knowing I could truly spit blood in any quarter of the universe. That was the moment in which I had last seen Hille, and no nostalgic erections could change it. So I followed her to the doctor's office on Queen Street, I had a hard time deciding which of these conflicting memories was not real, and finally gave up.

That's where she went — to the doctor's. I couldn't see any bandages, and she didn't seem to have anything broken; but that's where she went. To the doctor's.

Left following her then, and went back to Frederick Street where I put in two blistering hours shopping for a suit. Finally chose one at a Jew store. And I chose well. It caught my eye first thing as I entered, but I made the clerk show me every suit in the shop that was my size. Then when I was sure it was without comparison I bought the white doeskin. Doeskin flannel. White and soft as the first hairs on a baby rabbit. 'Nothing look better than that on you,' the clerk said. He was right. The shoulders make me look just a shade broader, and the pants, just full enough so nobody could tell whether I'm skinny or fat once I'm in them. He tried to sell me some shoes too, and a hat, but I didn't want any of those. That tender white doeskin tickling the backs of my legs and arms was enough. Especially when I didn't have to buy a suit. Especially when I had no business buying a suit. The purchase left me just change from seventy-two dollars, but it was a great moment when the Jew handed me back the few coins, and I strode out into the blistering heat with the suit neatly packaged under my arm. Let old Inspector come now! He drives up up to my door, I stop him coolly — 'Wait a minute. Just one minute.' Then I step back inside and I change — and he could stand there looking at me in my underdrawers if he likes — put on my white doeskin, and see the lapels are laying down right, then, 'Very well, Inspector.'

Then after I had been walking for a long time I wanted to see my boys — suddenly, badly, I wanted to see them. I had wandered a long ways from downtown, wandered up to beyond the Savannah where I suddenly found myself at the foot of the hills. I had no intention of going into the hills, and they weren't especially asking me up either. They stood there like giant woolly-headed bishops. I turned my back on them, reawakened to the feeling for my boys, and soon found myself wandering along that street in the city which is lined with foreign embassies. What stately buildings! What ornate grounds! And each building, verandah or no, standing in its own quaint garden, quiet and reserved under its fluttering flag. There were no rain clouds in the sky. 'Thanks for a clear day,' I heard myself mutter, quite as if the wide light did have something to do with me wandering along this quiet street with my new suit wrapped in brown paper under my arm. Sometimes on Saturdays in the village I used to watch a servant or gardener approach Anthony's father's house looking for a job. Seldom did they walk right up and enter the yard. They passed it one way, and then the next, and if they had a parcel under one arm they had to set it down in the grass beside the driveway, and squat there for a moment too, and if another man went by, or even if Anthony's father drove up in his jitney he did not disturb them because they had to be left alone, feeling for the right moment to get up and approach the overseer's door. But there was no flag flying above Anthony's father's house. This street of embassies though was lined with the fluttering rags, and once I read somewhere about Ivanhoe wandering into a place where there were rows of tents beneath just such flags — but of course those tents of long ago could be no match for the buildings along this street, except for the candy stripe colours and ornate fringes, perhaps. Thanks for a clear day that was into afternoon with still not a cloud climbing over the hills. Thanks for a clear day in which I may lie back under the linden shade on the brink of the wide empty green savannah. Heat waves in the distance. Shimmering coils of heat going upwards, upward, getting lost against the pastel horizon, and at the zenith, all those brave flags fluttering above the foreign houses. That's what this world was all about — flags. Uruguay, Colombia, Ethiopia, Germany, and England and Spain and France! Ethiopia? I couldn't tell — maybe they were all there. And Brazil, Argentina, and Canada. Ethiopia? I really couldn't tell. Egypt? We were too far from the Suez Canal. The Nile never flowed into the Atlantic. I really couldn't tell what all flew up there — they were flags. And foreign. And someone brought them across the seas. Someone brought them here, maybe flying from the steady masts of ships across many days like this one — blue and clear, with a pastel horizon and frothy waves lapping at the bows. Ships. They brought everything here. And everybody. I never did think to make that clear to my boys. Without ships, no Columbus, no Raleigh, no Hood, nor Don Chacon, no Toussaint, scalags, slaves, nor coolies. None of it. None of us. And he who invented ships held the key to the universe. Did he intend for them to stink? Who invented the ship? Columbus? Don't be a fool. The Phoenicians plied their oars centuries before Columbus found his way to Spain. Amerigo de Vespucci? Don't be ridiculous. The Egyptians were paddling themselves up and down the Nile before the Romans ever learned about water. The Vikings? Even before them. And before them. And before them. Give up? No one knows who invented the ship. Some say Noah, but no one really knows, because whoever he was had many faces, many names, and he came from many lands simultaneously. Whoever he was he left us a cipher to the universe and we've been struggling to unlock its secret ever since. That sounds good. But you can't bullshit children. Of course I mean we! All of us are here because of ships! No, I've never been on a ship. I've never been on the water except that day we rode out from Carenage. But I know what ships are like. I feel them up my bones. I know the dip and rise, the constant wash and spray, the vomit and groans of the sick, the chains, and the wailing in the dark holds, the waiting, bruised, strangling from the fetid odours of hundreds like me, waiting for what new land up ahead. And what new life. Life? Well we are still searching. No, I'll never make a voyage under such conditions again. I'll never leave the tropics so scantily clad I must cringe from the cold of the North Sea.

As if I would ever make any sort of trip at all!

Anthony was the one for whom ships and travelling were a reality. He was the one who knew just how to sneak Cleo aboard. It was not all dreaming with him, he had been on a ship. His family, his ancestors, had been for ages masters of ships, so it was nothing strange to find himself at age six propped up on the bow of the great iron liner cutting south, then west. 'What was it like?' 'Oh, I hardly remember. There was a lot of wind.' 'Did you get sick? People say you always get sick the first time you ride a boat.' 'We weren't riding a boat. It was a liner, taller than the house you live in. I don't remember being sick, but mother was. Father walked Richard and me about the deck while she lay in the cabin.' 'Were you sorry to leave London?' 'We never were in London. We belong to Liverpool.' 'Is that like here — with a factory, and pond and everything?' 'There are factories in Liverpool, but I don't remember them. Maybe ponds too, I don't know. We never had one there. Mostly dark and wet — that's what I remember of Liverpool, and sitting on a backyard step waiting for the sun.' 'Did it come?' 'Yes. But it never stayed long. Not like here. And you know what I remember too? sitting in the captain's chair on the liner. He, or dad, someone lifted me into his chair and put his cap on my head, and I knew he combed his hair with rosemary. His cap was strong with it. That almost made me sick.' 'When I get to be a man I'm going to take a ship and see the whole world.' 'You're dreaming.' 'No, really! When I get to be a man I'm going to take a big liner and go to London, go to Marseille, and Lisbon, Cadiz . . . ' 'I still say you're dreaming. Your family isn't rich enough for you to ever do all that.' 'My grandfather is from Barbados, and he's been up and down the Main on ships.' 'Your grandfather was a slave.' 'No he wasn't. He was born in 1860.' 'Well, that makes him only a little bit not a slave. Did he really travel the Main?' 'Sure. He's even been to Carthagena.' 'Slave families never had any money. How did he do it?' 'Work. The same way I'm going to do it. Only the ships I take are going to be bigger and better than Grandfather's.' 'Well, I don't care about your grandfather. The person I care about is Cleo.' 'Me too.' 'As soon as I'm finished with school . . . '

'Black, white,' The Undertaker said to me, 'they're all the same.' That was all. After I had been talking to him for practically the whole afternoon. Black, white — they're all the same. 'I see it all the time,' he went on. 'White ones, black ones, all the same. Before they're dead too — that's what a lot of men don't realize.'

'Yes,' I said.

'She went upstairs just now, you know.'

'Yes. I saw her.'

'You were so busy remembering about Betty I didn't know whether you had or not.'

'Yes, I saw her go up.'

'Smooth eh! Smooth. Every time I catch her legs on those steps going up my eyes say "smooth all the way". Eh? Boy you ought to bring her roses and teach her how to dance. Want to borrow my Benny Goodman? He is the king of jazz you know.'

'Well . . . ' all the time thinking; not all the time, but suddenly thinking, where was Prez, and Bird, and Diz? Good man must be a lie. There's no such body. After all the jazz I've heard too (that's one thing the war did for radio in Trinidad) I know jazz is moaning and groaning. Shit and blood and scornful sperm. Listen to it, overhear (maybe underhear) all the bloods and sperms of our New World swallowing on each other, trying each its best to do a clean job of it. No stains. And I'd like to say once, say-shout, ENOUGH. MY GOD, ENOUGH! Can we please now move on? MAY WE? PLEASE? I know grandmammy lost whatever her pants were supposed to protect, and grandpappy got so tired of losing his he after a while started pretending he didn't have anything up behind his cloth. Wailing, and pretending, and bragging, and easy death. Not bragging, bragga-docioing, and easy death. Enduring till easy death. I DON'T WANT TO DIE. ' . . . well, let me see if she likes him first.' I don't have to die. Nor pretend I'm dead to live. That is, I don't want to pretend I'm dead to live. So, tell me quick. After the giddy Saturday nights and nauseous Sunday mornings, and the blood-sucking weekdays, tell me something else. Like, how in the face of all this shit can I be a Good man? I really want to know. Tell me. Where is this Good man? Where is he at? Tell me about him. What's he doing? Tell me about him quick, because he's the one who knows the most about no-dying. Tell me about him, tell me how he is no lie. Yes, I know. Vulgar to occupy your time with such irrelevant enquiries. I know. Irrelevant emotionalisms, vulgar, primitive! And above all, primitive is the last word on the non-civilized, the not-worth-your-precious-time, except as something to stir vague apprehensions. I know. Truth is, you couldn't tell me about the Good man anyway. Isn't that right? His whereabouts, nothing — even if you had a mind to. Isn't that right? And it's a shame, but you have fooled around with hiding him from everybody so long, you don't know where he's at now yourself. Well . . . let me see if she likes him first. 'I'll let you know.' Truth is, you can't tell me shit. Isn't that right? Answer me brother. Why do undertakers have such nondescript voices anyway? You can't tell a damn thing! Isn't that right? and isn't it a bitch. Did I hear you say something? I am the unfinished conscience of mankind kicked out? Did you say that? Kicked out of the tribe so that it could get along with the business of progressing? No conscience — progress, is that it? But with a conscience, nobody knows? Because that hasn't been tried yet. And I'm to remain unfinished, are you saying? I am maintained unfinished — and so shall it be. For the day when I become finished there will be peace on earth, and in that very day an end to all mankind. ISN'T THAT RIGHT?

'Isn't what right? ISN'T WHAT RIGHT?' The voice ricocheting off my eardrums. But it was only Hille raised up on her skinny arms hanging over me, and repeating in mock singsong voice, 'Isn't what right?'

'Nothing,' I said.

'It's the first time I've heard you dreaming out loud.'

'I wasn't dreaming.'

'Then who were you screaming at, isn't that right?'

'Nobody.'

'You never tell me anything, Marcus. Tell me what you're thinking.'

'Nothing. I'm not thinking anything.'

She got then the look on her face which said she was about to whimper, and I had to stroke the back of her neck and say, 'Don't look like that, Hille, Everything's all right.'

'Why don't you talk plain?' she whimpered anyway.

Why don't you talk plain? A difficult thing to do when there is nothing to be said.

She came down again, her skin very hot and sticky. She seemed to have more bones than I remembered, seemed heavier too, but it would have been unkind to squirm and I didn't. Her shoulder right beneath my nose, I kissed it, salt-sweaty. I fingered the damp hairs about her neck; sweat all down her back, and in between us too. She had done all the work. Now

185

slumped down, waiting, on the edge of terror? despair? just plain giving-up-sadness seemed like, waiting, and me with not a word, not even an I love you. While, with a determined plunge her fingers locked into my crotch, saying, 'Let's go away Marcus. Let's go away.'

'Where?'

'I don't care. Anywhere.'

'Spain?'

'Yes.'

'Africa?'

'Yes.'

'And Marseille and Liverpool and Amsterdam and Carthagena?'

'Yes yes yes, everywhere. Anywhere you want to go. I'll get us passage.'

'Can't.'

'Can't what? Of course I can get us passage to anywhere we want to go. And if Daddy doesn't come through, I have money of my own. I'll work ... '

'That's not what I mean.'

'Can't what then?'

'Can't go. I can't go. The Inspector ... '

'Godamn the Inspector,' she said, springing to her knees in the bed. 'He can't keep you from leaving.'

'Yes he can.'

'Damn it, he can't. Not if you really want to go.'

Coming back with a feeble, 'He can.'

'Damn you. Goddamn you! Nothing has changed. Not a thing ... ' Crying for real now, the damp matted hair falling over her ears and down past her crimping mouth. Ugly. 'Goddamn you! A man's dead, and for all we know I'm carrying your child right now, and you're telling me ... what're you telling me? What do you want me to do?'

'What man's dead?'

'You killed him. You killed him.'

'What man's dead?'

'Murderer! You black sonofabitching murderer! I'll tell the police you killed him. So help me God. I'll tell the police you killed him with your bare hands.'

It was too much of an effort to take her neck this time, so I didn't. But closed my eyes without saying — it was my fault but we shouldn't have done this. My fault because I shouldn't have followed you into the bed. Was it then really my fault? On the steps coming up from The Undertaker I had no such thought in mind. Had none whatever (thoughts) in mind, except what a sad-assed thing it was being an undertaker who believed flowers and Benny Goodman epitomized some statement or the other of love. Not even thinking of her as someone I love, seeing as how I have never thought of anybody that way. Until suddenly we were there in my very familiar room, but with an awkwardness upon us, and we weren't talking. I had already asked how she was and she had already replied fine. I had already said I had seen her going to the doctor's and she had said yes, I saw you following me. I was curious about why she had seen the doctor, but I did not ask.

'Don't you want to know why I went to the doctor?'

'Yes. What is the matter with you?'

'I had a haemorrhage.'

'Haemorrhage?'

'Yes. Right after the ... the ... accident. It went on for almost two days. I missed you terribly all the time, and I was afraid for what might be happening to you in jail.'

'Oh.' So we were back to blood. No smears on the face and hands this time, no stains on the shirt. But blood. A simple leak; blood leaking out. I understood about Anthony lying there with his blood running into the pickle juice over the floor. I remembered the confusion of voices led by Amerigo's, and the sight of blood coming slowly from Anthony's smashed nose and ear. Confusion of voices, pushing, stumbling, until ambulance guards, police, doctor, old redface, all had swiftly arrived and taken over the shop, and I was being bullied along to the police station. I did not see Hille go down. So what made her haemorrhage?

'I couldn't help it,' she said. 'It must have been the sight of his blood.'

'The sight of blood made you haemorrhage?'

'No, no. I fell. I fainted, I think. I couldn't help myself. Oh darling, didn't it look terrible? All that blood?'

'I don't remember.'

'His face was all smashed and bloody with teeth sticking through, and blood running from his ears. I've never seen anything like it before. They took me to the hospital right away and the doctor said I had a haemorrhage.'

'From fainting?'

'That's what he said.'

A silence then, while I pondered that — fainting and haemorrhage and fainting — but couldn't make sense out of the combination. Yet seeing as though I were there as she recounted, the black-handed guards lifting ever so gently the golden-haired angel into their chariot and whisking her off to the black-handed doctor who lifting her dress cautiously says 'Haemorrhage' and hands her back to the waiting attendants for a swift transfer to another doctor with white hands, who dabs away the blood and delivers a stern reprimand, before prescribing a sedative, and an injunction to 'see me once a week'.

'They saved my life,' she said, 'the doctor and those ambulance attendants.'

Yes, it must have been quite a ride from my village to the hospital, stretched out beside Anthony, unable to stop inhaling the scent of his blood. And who took care of his wounds? Seeing too, although she wasn't there, couldn't tell, the slower operation on him dead on arrival, slow and solemn, a removal to his father's private suite, bathing and bandaging, and making ready for his last appearance.

'I am very sorry I lost it,' she said.

'What?'

'I said I'm sorry,' stroking my arm. 'I'm very sorry that I lost it.'

What she's getting at coming closer now, and a subtle part of me saying Grandfather was right about women. Their flesh is always their flesh. 'Well it doesn't make much difference now,' I said.

'Yes it does. That was our love's labour lost Marcus, and it was my fault.'

'Why should you want my bastard child?'

'Don't talk about it like that. It wouldn't be a bastard. We could get married right away — but even if we didn't do that it wouldn't be a bastard. It would be our love child. Yours and mine. Our love child . . . ' stroking my arm and laying such moist eyes upon me there was not much else to do but put an arm about her. 'Our love child, Marcus. Yours and mine.'

I must admit that the warmth of her breasts burned me, her little flat belly too, so even though I had already done with her I did not resist being ushered to bed, where she undressed and undressed me and did all the work without frenzy or sweetness, with just a great cavernous suck as though the Haemorrhage had left her very empty indeed.

And I must have dozing returned to my talk with The Undertaker, to be roused by her saying, 'Isn't what right?'

I had made another mistake, but that was all right. I was under control.

I didn't take her neck in my hands but lay back with my eyes closed, let her dress without interruption, listened to her stomp down the steps 'on my way to the police'.

Well, she's gone. Hille's gone now and I can rest in peace as long as I don't think about Betty — who really will have a child. Anthony's bastard.

Only two things left to do now — spread out my suit, and wait for the Inspector's coming. The hell with what they overheard downstairs. I have offered enough explanations.

Like the old Reverend-tutor once said, life never makes any noise — it goes about its business silently, deep and intensely, and without looking back. The trick still remains to convince oneself that losing is winning.